"Where are you running off to?" he asked.

"Nowhere," she said, turning to face him. Her expression—her eyes wide, her lips parted slightly, full and inviting—drew him in closer. "I just needed some air."

"Dancing with Bastian had such a strong effect on you?" he asked, advancing further.

She turned her head, casting her face into shadow. Her expression was obscured. "No. It had no effect on me. As usual. But it was more disturbing this time since the date of my official engagement is set now. And he's very likely the one I'll be engaged to. If his bid is high enough. I've been too cowardly to ask what the price is on my head—or hand, as the case may be."

"You want to feel attraction for him?"

"I want something. Anything."

Makhail stopped right in front of her, noticed a shimmer in her dark eyes, pale moonlight reflected there, betraying the depth of her emotion. He put his hand on her face. Just to offer comfort, just for a moment. There was no harm in that.

The feel of her smooth skin beneath his palm sent a shock of desire through him. Strong. Foreign. Intense. It was almost enough simply to feel that need. To revel in it. The desire of a man for a woman. Almost.

Maisey Yates was an avid Mills & Boon® Modern™ Romance reader before she began to write them. She still can't quite believe she's lucky enough to get to create her very own sexy alpha heroes and feisty heroines. Seeing her name on one of those lovely covers is a dream come true.

Maisey lives with her handsome, wonderful, diaper-changing husband and three small children across the street from her extremely supportive parents and the home she grew up in, in the wilds of Southern Oregon, USA. She enjoys the contrast of living in a place where you might wake up to find a bear on your back porch and then heading into the home office to write stories that take place in exotic urban locales.

Recent titles by the same author:

ONE NIGHT IN PARADISE
GIRL ON A DIAMOND PEDESTAL
HAJAR'S HIDDEN LEGACY

Did you know these are also available as eBooks?
Visit www.millsandboon.co.uk

A ROYAL WORLD APART

BY
MAISEY YATES

First published in Great Britain 2012
by Mills & Boon, an imprint of Harlequin (UK) Limited.
Harlequin (UK) Limited, Eton House, 18-24 Paradise Road,
Richmond, Surrey TW9 1SR

© Maisey Yates 2012

ISBN: 978 0 263 22751 2

A ROYAL WORLD APART

To Megan Crane and Paula Graves. It was our Twitter conversation that inspired me to write Mak.

And to my fabulous editor Megan Haslam, who always helps bring out the best in me.

CHAPTER ONE

THE scandalous princess had done it again. Evangelina Drakos had slipped away from yet another one of his top security guards. It was inexcusable. It was something that should never happen. And yet, it had. Three times in as many weeks.

Makhail Nabatov did not tolerate mistakes. Mistakes, no matter how small—from losing the princess one was meant to be guarding, down to the simple act of spilling hot coffee on yourself while driving—could be disastrous.

He slammed his car door and rolled his shoulders forward, trying to ease the tension that had every muscle in his body bound into knots as solid as stone. He didn't believe in letting anything affect him like this. Yet another way Princess Evangelina seemed to be messing with the carefully well-ordered life he maintained.

When he'd met her for the first time, all glossy brown curls, dark, glittering eyes and golden skin, she had seemed every inch the demure princess. Nothing like the bold, vivacious party girl who was making tabloid headlines with increasing frequency. He had wondered if the media had exaggerated her image.

Over the past six months he'd discovered that the tabloids were right, and he was wrong. He was never wrong. And yet the Drakos princess had proven him so.

He didn't like it.

It defied logic that one petite royal could cause so much trouble. And yet, this one seemed to have a knack for it.

He punched the speed dial on his phone for the man he'd had watching out for the princess. "Ivan, where did you last see her?"

"The casino. She disappeared into the crowd," Ivan said, his voice filled with fear. More weak emotion. He despised it.

"You're fired." Makhail clicked the end-call button and stuffed the phone back into his pocket, straightening his tie before striding down the electric strip of the only major city on the island of Kyonos. He was willing to bet Evangelina was still in the casino. Gambling away her father's money, no doubt.

He moved seamlessly through the crowd, weaving past revelers on his way through the gilded doors. Princess Evangelina wouldn't be in the main entry trying her hand at the slots. He'd bet she was in one of the high-roller rooms. It was the only place in a casino for a spoiled brat with a penchant for drama and pink champagne.

He passed quickly through the lobby and headed toward a pair of black doors in the back, flanked on either side by guards in suits.

"Name?" One of the men asked.

"Mak," he said. "I'm here to see the princess."

"I'm afraid you can't just…"

One of the doors opened and a socialite in a skin-tight dress breezed out, the scent of alcohol clinging to her body. He took advantage of the moment and gripped the edge of the door, pulling it open the rest of the way and walking in.

He spotted her right away, bent over the table, laughing as she watched the man to her right roll a pair of dice, cheering when the numbers came up favorably. Then she looked up, at him.

Her dark eyes rounded, her pink lips parting slightly. She

touched her companion's arm and said something quickly before edging away from him. She wasn't trying to run, not from him. She knew better than that.

One of the guards rushed into the room and everyone looked up from the game. "Princess," he said, "is everything…?"

She regarded Mak cooly, her manner distant, disdainful. "I would prefer it if this man wasn't here, but trust me when I say there's no way you can remove him," she said crisply. "He's in the employ of my father. You can see that that could become problematic." Her tone was commanding, haughty. Her dark eyes glittered with anger, proving her collected tone of a voice to be a lie. "So, I'm to be taken back to my cell then?"

"Your cell?" he asked. "Is that what you call that frilly pink bedroom of yours?"

A hint of raspberry color touched her golden cheeks. "Not officially."

"How did you lose your tail?"

Her lips curved upward into a smug smile. "Did you see the women at the slot machines in front? The ones who make change for patrons?"

He shook his head once. "No."

"Ah. Well, your guard did. Or more specifically, he noticed the fact that the necklines of their dresses were cut down to their navels. I took the opportunity to slip in back. He must have assumed I'd gone out front, as he'd suggested."

Mak clenched his teeth. "He was deluded. Naive enough to believe you would do as commanded."

Evangelina raised her eyebrows, her expression overly innocent. "Indeed."

"I am not."

One side of her mouth quirked upward. "I noticed."

He regarded her for a moment. She had a feline quality to her. Lithe, graceful and more than ready to bare her claws if the need presented itself. He could see how she'd managed to intimidate the palace guards, how she'd managed to dupe his men.

She would not do the same to him.

"I would recommend, *printzyessa*, that you come with me."

"And if I don't?"

"Your father will hear of this," he said.

She crossed her arms beneath her breasts. Now, *her* breasts he noticed. She wasn't showing off every bit of skin she could get away with and still be considered dressed. And it made her figure all the more enticing for it. It made him wonder. Made him wonder if she was golden all over. Made him wonder what her breasts would look like, uncovered for him.

He clenched his hands into fists, battling the images that flashed through his mind. He didn't let women distract him. Ever.

This was an aberration. As unusual as it was unwanted. It would not happen again.

"I'm not all that concerned over my father hearing about this. What will he do? Lock me in the dungeon? Or perhaps he'll marry me off to a stranger at his convenience? We both know he won't do the former, and he's actively attempting to accomplish the latter."

"I'll throw you over my shoulder and carry you out. If your designer heels don't make it…" he shrugged, "it's not my problem."

Her dark eyes narrowed. "You wouldn't."

He took a step toward her. She didn't shrink, didn't step away. "You don't think?"

She regarded him for a moment. "I'll allow you to escort me out."

He reached out and took hold of her arm, running his fingers over her smooth skin, her flesh hot beneath his palm. He pulled her to him, linking their arms. He leaned in, his lips brushing her ear. "*I* will allow you to leave on your own two feet."

She turned to face him, deep brown eyes blazing with defiance. "Good for both of us, as I imagine the alternative would not have ended well. For you *or* for me."

"Then it's good you chose the right option." He held tightly to her arm, leading her from the room. She kept her chin tipped up, her neck craned, likely so she could look down her nose. It gave her a haughty, untouchable air. It made all of the men in the room practically fall at her feet.

They breezed through the foyer and back out into the damp night air. Salt spray lingered, thick and pungent and the sound of the sea could be heard roaring in the distance. He opened the passenger door to his car.

"In," he commanded.

She complied, stiffly, her posture rigid as she settled into the vehicle, her eyes fixed straight in front of her. He rounded the car and got into the driver's side, revving the engine and pulling away from the curb, heading in the direction of the palace.

"So," she said, her voice conversational, "you won't tell my father?"

"No." It wouldn't benefit anyone to bring the king into this.

"I might tell him," she said, her tone still light, casual. Obnoxious.

"Why is that?"

"As I said, he won't do anything about it. He has no leverage. At least, as far as what he can do to *me*. Now you... he may fire you."

Makhail tightened his grip on the steering wheel. "He won't."

"Really?"

"No. He won't. I fired Ivan, and now I personally will be

guarding you. Your father knows that there isn't anyone better suited to the job."

"Does he?" she said, her tone flat.

"Your palace guards can't keep tabs on you, and they cannot be distracted from issues of national security to deal with
a brat who has no interest in her own safety. That leaves me. I
am in the unique business of guarding royalty when the built-
in protection of a nation proves to be ineffective. And I never
make mistakes. It's regrettable that one of my employees did."

"Two," she said.

"What?"

"Two of your employees did." She reinforced the figure
by holding up a matching number of fingers. "I've given two
of them the slip while they were busy rubbernecking some
woman's figure."

"Former," he said.

"What?"

"Former employees. They lacked discipline, and that
means I have no room for them among my staff. You may
not realize this, as your spoiled tendencies keep you from
looking too far outside of yourself, but this is about more
than image."

"Is it? I thought it was mainly about making sure I didn't
look unsuitable to possible fiancés."

"This is about your safety. You are an important piece of
political power, *printzyessa*."

"Am I?" She injected false, breathless surprise into her
voice. "And here I thought I was just Evangelina."

"When a title is involved, no one is 'just' anything."

She turned to face him, the indicator the sound of her
clothes sliding over the leather. He didn't turn to look at her.
Didn't take his eyes of the road. "Except I am. I am *just* a
political pawn."

"An important one," he said.

She snorted and he heard her flop back against her seat. "What more could a girl ask for?"

Eva felt as though she was going to crawl out of her skin. Her arm still burned from where Makhail had touched her, and she was so angry she thought she might actually fold in on herself. Yes, she was being outrageous and she knew it. But it was her power. Her only power.

Impotent, it turned out.

Six months ago, when her father had introduced her to Makhail she'd breathed a sigh of relief that he was no longer a field agent. That he wouldn't be guarding her personally. Because he…well, he was just too disturbing. Far too big. Too masculine. Broad shoulders and cropped brown hair, a square jaw, a mouth that looked as if it had never smiled. And his eyes…gray like the barrel of a gun. And they were every bit as cold.

And now here he was. It was one thing to mess around his goons. Easy too. They were far too interested in what was going on around them. But Makhail focused in on her in a way that no one else ever did. It was as if he was looking into her. She didn't like it at all.

"Perhaps a girl could ask for more diamonds in her gilded cage?"

"You think because I'm rich I have no right to complain?" she asked.

"Not at all. I'm not here to have an opinion. An opinion would imply that I care. I don't. I am here to do a job. Keep you safe, keep you scandal-free. I will do it."

"Until my marriage?"

"After, if I must."

A strange thought. That she would be guarded even after her marriage was secured, and yet she knew it was true. She was a royal, destined to marry a royal. From the moment she'd been born, her life had been controlled down to what shoes she was to put on in the morning.

And of course, the man she would marry was also to be carefully selected. Just like her breakfast cereal.

It had been over six months since she'd woken up to a terrible, clawing fear that she would never be able to make a decision for herself. Not one. Not about what she wore, not about where she went, or what she ate. That was when the serious rebellion started. So Makhail Nabatov could talk about duty and spoiled brattiness all he wanted, but he didn't know what it was like to be her.

He was the enemy.

"I dare say my husband will have his own guards intent on ensuring my submission."

"And what makes you think they'll be any better than your father's guards?"

He didn't look at her, never took his eyes from the road, his profile strong, uncompromising. A crooked nose that looked as though it had been broken at least once, a square jaw that verged on being too sharp. A mouth that looked incapable of smiling.

"They may not be. But maybe I won't try to escape. That all depends on who my father selects, I suppose. Or if I fall in love with him."

She doubted she would. She had a vague idea of who her father might find suitable, because there weren't very many royals just lying around for her to marry. A few minor members of nobility, and of course there was Bastian, King of Komenia, a small principality in eastern Europe, actively looking for his queen. She felt nothing for him, no matter how hard she tried. And she did try.

Because he was the likeliest candidate. The one who would bring the most strength, the most power, financial and military resources to Kyonos.

How she felt—love, attraction—didn't come into it as far as her father was concerned. And Bastian was nice. He was even rather handsome. But there was no spark. He touched her and she felt nothing. He wasn't the one.

But it was looking as though she would never have the chance to find that man.

"You want love, do you?" he asked, maneuvering the car through the narrow streets, café tables pressed in so close to the roadway that if she rolled the window down she could reach out and steal a cappuccino. Unless of course the windows were locked. Likely, under the circumstances.

"Of course I do. Don't we all?"

"No," he said. No explanation, just no. She wasn't sure why she was surprised. Except she was. And then it made her angry. Because he could have love if he wanted it. He could marry whomever he wanted to, and he didn't have anyone trying to make the decision for him.

But he just…said no, he didn't want love. Probably because he was more interested in cleavage, anonymous cleavage, than he was in a real woman. That was what she'd noticed with the other men who guarded her. That was how she'd shaken them.

Makhail was no different, though he was more focused when he needed to be, clearly, since he hadn't even noticed the busty cocktail waitresses at the entrance of the casino.

But still, he had all the freedom in the world and he wanted to waste it on shallow, frivolous things. Not that her night in the casino had been anything more than shallow and frivolous. But it had been fun, and she'd had a shortage of fun in her life.

"Well. I do," she said, looking out the window again, her stomach tightening as they neared the palace.

"Why?"

"What do you mean *why*?" She turned to his profile again.

"Everyone—well, not you, we established not you—most everyone wants love. Love is…"

"A lot of work."

She looked down at his hands, his grip tight on the steering wheel. There was a platinum band there, thick and prominent, on his left ring finger. "Are you married?"

"Not anymore," he said. There was no emotion in his voice. No hint of how he felt about the subject. Yet he still wore his ring.

"Why?"

He flicked her a glance for the first time. "I did not realize we had to become friends in order for me to protect you."

"Let's get one thing straight," she said, annoyance coursing through her. "You aren't protecting me. Not really. You're keeping me out of trouble. Or perceived trouble. I'm an adult woman. I'm twenty, you know. Almost twenty-one."

"Ancient," he said, his tone dry.

"Anyway, no, we don't have to be friends. I suppose us being friends would be impossible, actually, seeing as we're working with opposing agendas."

"And what is your agenda, Princess?"

They pulled up to a wrought-iron gate, guards stationed out along the perimeter of the pale stucco wall that stretched around the palace, backed by the Aegean Sea.

"If I told you, Mr. Nabatov, it would be much too easy for you to gain the upper hand."

CHAPTER TWO

"It was online, on every trashy news website you could think of, before you ever left the casino, Eva." Her father paced in front of her, his hands locked behind his back, his expression fierce. "Rolling dice, men on your arm. You looked like a common college student."

An insult from her father's lips. There was no mistaking that. Anything common, as far as Stephanos Drakos was concerned, was beneath the hallowed royal family of Kyonos.

"Father..."

"Your Highness," Makhail stepped in, his voice smooth, confident. "Eva was meant to be under the supervision of one of my men, who has been dismissed now for his carelessness. I have decided I will take on the task of guarding the princess myself."

Bloody gallant of him. So gallant she'd like to smack that smug expression right off his face. Instead, she cleared her throat and addressed her father. "I don't suppose you've considered that I don't need twenty-four-hour...nannying?"

"Not for a moment," King Stephanos replied.

Makhail turned to her, his gray eyes glinting. "I am not a nanny, Princess."

"You do carry a bigger gun than most nannies," she said.

He arched one brow. "Among other things."

"Charming," she said tightly.

"How do I know I can trust you, Mr. Nabatov, when you seem incapable of keeping an agent in my daughter's presence?"

Makhail turned his focus to the king, his expression hard. Fierce. Almost frightening. "They were fools. I am not. And your options are limited, Your Highness. Typically, when we protect someone, they have the good sense to want that protection. Princess Evangelina does not."

"That's because I'm being protected from myself," she said. "It's insulting."

"You behave like a child, and you shall be treated like one," Stephanos said. "I am in the process of arranging a union for you that will benefit Kyonos, benefit your people. You disdain it."

"I…I just want to have a bit of my own life…a bit of…"

"You are royal, Eva. It is not that simple," the king said.

Eva bit back her response. Because, as much as she hated it, he was right. Every privilege, every ball, had a price. Every ounce of gold dust came with a twenty-pound iron weight attached to it. It didn't matter whether she accepted it, it simply was.

Still, the outright refusal burned in her throat. Desperate to escape. Words she knew she could never speak.

"Am I dismissed?" she asked.

"You may go," her father said, nodding his head.

She turned on her heel and walked out into the hall, covering her face with hands, digging the heels of her palms into her eyes, trying to keep tears from falling. She wasn't weak. She didn't have time for weakness. Even more importantly, she couldn't afford to show it.

Not to her father, certainly not to the press. Least of all to Makhail, her brand-new jailer. The only person who understood her, even a little bit, was Stavros, her brother. And at the moment, he had his own problems.

She stalked down the long, empty corridor of the palace, making each step count, her high heels clicking loudly on the marble floor. If she had any idea what she wanted, things would be so much easier.

Making scandal, derailing her father's plans to find her a suitable husband, that had kept her busy for the past few months, but she had no end plan with it.

What else could she do?

She knew what she wanted. She also knew she would probably never have it. A man who loved her, just her. A man she loved just as madly in return. A marriage that had nothing to do with politics or trade.

It was nothing more than a fantasy. Some little girls dreamed of being princesses. She'd just dreamed of being. Of living on her own terms, making her own goals, goals she could aspire to. It wasn't possible, but she'd clung to the hope. For too long.

And any freedom she had had a timer ticking on it. The marriage was being arranged. And when she was married… it would all be gone, any hope squashed beneath the weight of it. She would go from being beneath her father's control to being beneath her husband's.

It was bleak.

"Princess."

The deep, rich voice, flavored by a Russian accent, could only belong to one man. She turned and saw Makhail standing there, looking every inch the secret agent in his black suit.

"Yes?"

"I have finalized arrangements with your father."

"Have you?" she asked, stiffly.

"He says you have six months."

She tried to ignore the sick, sinking feeling in her stomach. "So I've been sentenced, then?"

"Is that how you feel about it?"

She laughed, and she wasn't sure why. She didn't feel amused. Far from it. "How would you feel? Being offered as commodity to a total stranger? To bear his children and... sleep with him."

"I imagine I would not enjoy it," he said, his tone wry. "But then, I have never been interested in sleeping with men."

"You know what I meant."

"Listen, Princess..."

"Eva. Just Eva, please. If we have to deal with each other for the next few months it will be easier."

"Then you can call me Mak." It wasn't a friendly offer. More like a prisoner exchange.

"I don't want to," she returned, keeping her tone intentionally tart.

He chuckled. "Why is that?"

She crossed her arms beneath her breasts. "It humanizes you. I would prefer to stay angry with you for as long as possible."

His lips curved into a smile, one that didn't quite reach his eyes. He took a step, then another, slowly circling around her, like a predator who had found some very tempting prey. "I am certain I will find many ways to make you angry, Eva. You won't need to manufacture reasons."

"On that we can both agree." She turned to face him as he moved to her side. "Stop circling me, I'm not a gazelle."

He paused. "Excuse me?"

"You look like...like you're stalking me or something. But I am no one's prey."

"I believe it."

"Tell me then, Mak," she said his name with as much disdain as she could muster. "What is on the agenda? Has my father lined out every single activity I'm approved for over the six months? Galas and tea parties?"

"Something like that."

"Lovely," she said dryly.

"Not for either of us and I see no reason to pretend otherwise. I am not a babysitter, so unless you want me to be incredibly irritable during our time together, I suggest you stop acting like a child."

She stiffened, anger coursing through her veins, her temper, quick at the best of times, ready to snap. "I am not acting like a child. I'm being treated like one."

"What do you think, Eva, that you'll find the answers to life in a casino? In a bar? That somehow that sort of freedom means more than doing your duty to your country? If so, you really are a child."

He turned his back to her and for some, strange reason, she felt compelled to ask him to stay. To make him stay. "Wait."

He turned back to her. "Yes?"

"Where are you staying? Do you...do you have a home on Kyonos?"

"I shall be staying here." He smiled slowly. "All the better to protect you."

"Are you supposed to remind me of the big bad wolf?"

He arched one dark eyebrow. "Do I?"

Come to think of it, he did. "What big teeth you have," she said, forcing her voice to stay in a monotone.

His dark eyebrow arched. "I won't say the rest. It would hardly be appropriate."

A little thrill zinged through her. It certainly would not. And what was happening? Had he...flirted with her? Had she just flirted with her bodyguard?

He was gorgeous. In a very understated sort of way. He certainly wasn't pretty, he was far too rugged for that. But he was...masculine. And somehow, just being near him, made her feel very, very aware of her own femininity. Dark stubble shadowed his jaw and she imagined it would feel rough beneath her palm.

She found herself brushing her fingertips lightly over her own cheek in response to the thought, feeling the smooth skin there. Craving its opposite.

She dropped her hand to her side, flexing her fingers, trying to get rid of the phantom impression of his scruff, and took a deep breath, attempting to clear her head.

"Hardly," she said, trying to swallow. Her throat felt tight. Too tight.

"This doesn't have to be hard, Eva," he said, his accent shaping her name differently than she'd ever heard it before. It was…intriguing.

"It can't be anything but. You and I have opposing goals, Mak."

"What is your goal, Princess?" he asked, his eyes hard on her. Far too perceptive. He made her want to wrap her arms around herself, to try and cover as much as she could. Because she felt as though he could see beneath her filmy dress. More disturbing, she felt that he could see inside of her. See her fears, her desires. Things she'd never shared with anyone. "And be honest. None of this talk about you not telling me. Do you intend to take yourself out of the running for a dynastic marriage by ruining your image?"

"It had crossed my mind. Or perhaps, I simply wanted to start as I intend to go on."

"Meaning?"

"The lucky royal who takes me as a wife should have an idea of what he's getting into. He should know I'm not simply some docile piece of arm candy."

He treated her to that look again. Cool. Assessing. Penetrating. He spoke slowly, as though each word was chosen carefully. For the purpose of irritating her, she imagined. "I doubt anyone could possibly believe you're docile."

"Then my job is at least half done," she said, trying to play it a whole lot cooler than she felt. "I'm tired now. I think I'll go to my quarters." She turned away from him and started walking back down the hall.

She could hear heavy footfalls behind her. She turned and saw Mak following behind her. "I said I'm going to my quarters. You aren't invited," she said, even as her stomach tightened, thinking of inviting him in.

"I'm simply ensuring you arrive as you should," he said, completely unperturbed by her prickly responses. She was usually very good at putting her guards off. The palace guards had given up on her, Makhail's guards hadn't been able to keep up with her.

And Makhail was…calm. Maddeningly so. As though he felt nothing. Nothing more than a mild amusement over the disaster area that was her life. As though the idea of her being sold into marriage was nothing.

"Think I'm going to knot the bedsheets together and rappel out the window?"

"You've done it before."

Heat rushed into her cheeks. "Once. And I was fourteen. Did you read my file? Oh, *theos,* have I got a file?" She'd never, ever felt more like one of her father's assets in her life. Not a person, a thing. A thing that was catalogued, like the antiquities, like the artifacts from the temples of Kyonos. She was another item from the royal collection.

"Of course you have a file. And considering you burn through guards at such an accelerated rate, it's a good thing too. It made it much easier for me to know you."

She gritted her teeth, tightening her hands into fists. "You can study that file all you like, read it cover to cover. You still won't know me." She turned her back on him and took short, quick steps down the hall, ignoring the sound of him still behind her.

When she reached the door to her quarters, her hands shook as she entered the code that would unlock the door.

"I make it my business to know people," Mak said. "I profile them. It makes it easier in this business if I understand human nature. You think you're so special that I can't figure you out?"

She turned to him, her heart raging in her chest. "I'm not a list of characteristics. I am a person. I..."

"You are spoiled. Selfish. Characteristics brought on by a life with every amenity you could possibly imagine—and some most people can not—at your fingertips. You feel persecuted while surrounded by luxury, because you know nothing else. Because you don't know what it is to go without food or shelter. Oh, I think I know you, Eva. Better than you know yourself, quite possibly."

His assessment made her feel ill. Made her tremble from the inside out. Was it so wrong to want more out of her life than being an object? She wasn't an artifact, which made being wrapped in silk and put on display boring and unsatisfying.

She sucked in a breath and met Mak's eyes, ignored the shiver that worked its way through her as she did. "You can continue to think all of that if you wish. Frankly, you underestimating me works to my benefit."

He chuckled, low and slow. "Perhaps you are simply *over*estimating yourself." He moved closer to her and her heart kicked into high gear. He leaned in, his palm pressed flat against the door to her rooms, his face so near hers she could hardly breathe. For one moment, it all stopped. There was only Mak, his face filling her vision, his scent teasing her. "Sleep well, *printzyessa*."

He pushed back from the door and turned away from her, walking down the hall, his abandonment leaving her cold. His recent nearness leaving her shaking.

"Bastard," she said, loud enough for him to hear.

He didn't turn. He just laughed.

She pushed the door open and closed it firmly behind her. This was a disaster. A nightmare. She'd been downgraded to a maximum-security playpen.

She hated that man. That ridiculous, gorgeous, awful man.

Eva toyed with the idea of climbing out the window. For all of two seconds. She didn't have anywhere she wanted to be, and frankly, it would be rebellion for rebellion's sake and that was just stupid.

The casino stuff, that night she'd gotten into one of Kyonos's most exclusive and racy nightclubs, that had been for the benefit of the press. And even though she'd lost her bodyguard detail, she'd been sure she was safe.

Sneaking out in the dead of night didn't have the same benefit.

She sank into the sofa that stretched across the entryway to her quarters, which was structured very much like a luxury apartment without a kitchen. It was a way for her to have privacy without actually having it. An illusion of independence.

She closed her eyes, her head resting on a plush white cushion. She could feel the noose tightening around her neck. Duty. Honor. She should care about both of those things more than she did.

She just wanted her own life.

And in her position, wanting that made her selfish, terrible when it would be seen as normal, responsible, for someone else to want to take control of their existence. It was also completely impossible.

CHAPTER THREE

Eva in her fitted black slacks, white blouse and long string of pearls that hung low, knotted beneath her breasts, was a very different Eva from the one he'd encountered the night before. With her glossy brown hair tamed into a sleek bun, her makeup light and subtle, she looked every inch the proper princess.

But he knew better. He could not get the image of her as she had been last night out of his mind. Angry, and more than a little bit hot. She had plagued his dreams. Another strange occurrence. Even in sleep he had control. It had been necessary, for so long, for him to have control in every way. And he had gone into a business that took that and used it, made the most of it.

He couldn't afford to lose it now.

He had been forced to take to the beach early in the morning, running until his lungs burned and his muscles shook, until he was certain the desire for her had been replaced by utter exhaustion. It was a technique he had used often in the past. It had not worked today.

"Good morning, Mak," she said, looking up from her breakfast, her tone telling him there was nothing good about seeing him at all. So, she wasn't so different from last night's Eva.

"Morning."

"What's on my agenda for the day?"

"You are housebound."

Her head snapped up, her expression fierce. "Is that the way it's going to be, then?"

"There is a ball coming up at the end of the month."

"Ah yes, a ball. What is the function of those balls do you suppose? To trot me out before potential suitors."

"And for women to parade themselves before your brother, right?"

"True. As long as Stavros is single there will be balls. And minor royals gagging to marry a future king."

"And your brother is as interested in marriage as you are, I take it?"

"Less." She looked up at him again and for the first time, he saw a vulnerability in her eyes. He also saw her beauty, beauty that was impossible to ignore. "Although he'll do it. And he'll do it without argument. That's how he is. He does what's best. Feeling…well, feeling never comes into it for Stavros. Is it really house arrest until I'm engaged? Is that my only option?"

"What is it you want, Eva?" He moved to the table and sat across from her. "Beyond creating scandal?"

"Something. Anything. A chance just to be myself for a while. A chance to have some freedom. To live."

He ignored the slight twinge in his chest. "Your life is different, Eva."

"Ah yes, I'm a princess. Which, ironically, means I have less control than your average person. Not more."

"I find it difficult to muster any sympathy for you."

"So…in lieu of that you plan on watching me eat breakfast?" she asked, finely groomed brow arched. She was stunning. A study in refined beauty. In another life, well, this same life, but a part of it that was so long ago it might as well not have existed, he never would have been able to speak to a woman like her. A woman of her station.

And yet, things had changed. He had found great success. And with every step in his professional life, with every dollar added to his bank account, more had been torn away from his heart, more of the things he loved stripped from him.

Now he was a billionaire. Self-made royalty. The most highly regarded man in his field. And in so many other ways he was bankrupt. He could relate in some ways to her, more strongly than she could imagine.

Still, she was here. She could use her legs, her mouth, her mind. She had so much, and she seemed to appreciate nothing.

"Breakfast, then maybe coffee out on the terrace? Lunch later. A thrilling day for us both."

She rolled her eyes, the expression making her look like a rebellious teenager. He wasn't that much older than her. Just nine years. It felt like so much more. "How can you stand this?"

"Simple. I'm getting paid to be here."

"You don't need the money."

"You're right about that."

"Then why?"

He shrugged. "I have nothing else to do, and I don't believe in an idle life. I have built my company from nothing, I have a reputation to protect, and I intend to do it. I see a job through to completion and I don't intend to stop now."

"Well, you might have chosen your life, Mak. But I didn't choose mine."

He laughed at that. Laughter was a rare thing in his life, yet Eva seemed to make him laugh more easily than most. Unintentionally of course. "I didn't choose my life, any more than you chose yours. But what I did was make something with it." No one, not a single person in history, would have chosen the path he'd walked, not knowing where it led. He was certain of that.

"But you said you didn't have to work…you…"

"I don't. But I choose to, because I believe in what I do. I started my business for the same reason anyone starts a business. To make money. I did. I kept going, I made more. And now I am here." He looked around the dining room, bright, with large windows that overlooked a turquoise sea. "I started a job here, and like every job I have ever started, I will see it through to the end. Honor, keeping my word, that's more important than money. Something I realize you don't understand."

"That's low," she said, pushing her plate back. "I get that you pride yourself on reading people," she looked up, her dark eyes blazing, clashing with his, "but you don't know me. And you won't until you're facing a future filled with nothing but endless…endless darkness. An eternity serving other people with no consideration to yourself."

His stomach tightened. Painfully. It was still so easy to find himself back at Marina's bedside in his mind. Watching her face, so lovely at one time, contorted with pain, her lips opening for silent screams her damaged mind wouldn't allow her to articulate. Then sometimes she would scream. Sometimes…

He stood, trying to ignore the raging of his heart. He couldn't afford an emotional reaction. Not now. Never.

"I will make you a deal, *printzyessa*. I won't assume to know you, so long as you don't presume to know where I've been in my life. There are other paths to walk down than the one you speak of. There is darkness you can't imagine. Darkness no light can cut through." He breathed in deeply, ignoring the stricken look on her face, finding a foothold in his control and taking it. "Are you through eating?"

"Yes." She stood too, a hint of curiosity mingling with the anger in her eyes.

"Then perhaps you wouldn't mind showing me the grounds of the palace?"

Eva couldn't even pretend to be happy about playing tour guide to Mak, particularly since she didn't believe, for one second, that he wasn't well-versed in everything pertaining to the Kyonosian palace and its grounds. He'd read *her* file after all.

"So, now that we've covered every wing of the palace, and half of the gardens, be honest with me," she said. "You already know about everything I've told you, don't you?"

His expression remained stoic as he studied the little alcove. It was on the far end of the gardens, shrouded by hedges, with lattice and grapevines arching over them like a domed ceiling, providing shade and privacy. The ground was covered in stone carved with scenes from ancient stories. It was a sacred place, one her family never seemed to have time for. But she'd always liked it.

"I've been over the schematics for the palace in detail, and of course I've walked the perimeter, both of the grounds and of the palace itself."

"This was just to keep me busy."

"The bodyguard equivalent to a nanny's cartoon," he said, his tone as stoic as his face.

She shot him her deadliest glare. "And now you're being an ass on purpose."

A small smile curved his mouth. "I have to make my own fun."

She studied him for a moment, the hard lines of his face. Hardness not even the slight show of humor softened. "You don't look like you care one way or the other about fun."

He looked at her, his gray eyes intense. "You're right. I don't."

Being on the end of that look, of those eyes, made her feel hot all over. "So…so you can't really understand my problem."

"Your problem?"

She swallowed. "Yes. The fact that I want a life. You can't understand it because you have no desire to have one of your own."

He paused for a long moment. "It's been a long time since I've had one. It doesn't mean I don't understand it."

More puzzles. He was a complex man. Hard on the surface, letting things glance off without even feeling them. He had erected a barrier between himself and the world, that much was obvious. He was able to talk to her, joke even and yet, it felt as though he was barely giving any of himself in the process. Makhail, who he really was, was hidden behind that thick stone barrier he'd erected. She had a feeling if she could ever get a look behind it, she would find a darkness that would consume her.

Because she could *feel* it. Could see it sometimes, in his eyes. As frightening as his surface image was, all of that hard muscle displayed to its best advantage by military-grade posture, it was the man beneath that scared her most.

And intrigued her. Made her breath grow short and her stomach get tight. Which was actually scarier than Mak himself.

"Then, if you can imagine it, why can't you try and understand instead of simply assuming I'm a spoiled brat?"

"Because it's not my job to do anything that goes beyond your protection."

"But…you can protect me without holding me prisoner. You can…"

"I don't work for you, Eva. That means it's very likely your suggestions are wasted."

Her stomach tightened. "You're right. I don't know why I bothered. You aren't any different from anyone else. From my father."

She turned and he caught her arm, his touch sending a blaze of heat through her, her skin on fire where his fingers met her flesh. "And that means?"

She sucked in a sharp breath, determined to keep her composure. Determined to stay strong. "You only care about yourself, and you can use me to further your own end. For my father, it's about Kyonos. For you, it's about the job. I'm a person, Mak. And I am sick to death of people forgetting that. Who has to go around reminding people that they aren't a thing?" Her voice broke and she was horrified by the weakness. She didn't show weakness. It accomplished nothing. It earned her even less respect than she already got. She cleared her throat. "That's why your guilt trips don't work. That's why I can't feel bad for wanting more."

She jerked her arm out of his grasp and walked away as quickly as she could, willing the tears that were forming in her eyes not to fall. She didn't cry. Ever. She wouldn't start now.

It was late when Eva decided to try and make her escape. She didn't know where she was going. She didn't care. But there was no way she was allowing Mak to think that he had all the power here, not even close.

She was a princess, and that ought to mean something. Shouldn't she have some sort of power? Some sort of say in any part of her life?

She tightened the belt on her black trench coat and opened the door to her chambers, her heart pounding. She didn't usually sneak out of the palace. Usually, she conned her guard into taking her somewhere and sneaked off from there. But desperate times called for desperate measures.

She closed the door behind her as quietly as she could, her high heels dangling from her fingertips as she walked down the hall. The marble floor was cold on her feet, but it was preferable to announcing her presence with the click of her heels.

It was dark, and even though it was rare there wasn't some form of activity happening in the castle, everything was quiet in her wing. She could only hope that there wasn't anyone loitering in the halls.

She rounded the corner and hit a hot, solid barrier. A hand over her mouth cut off her sharp shriek, strong arms turning her sharply, putting her back to the wall. Her eyes clashed with Mak's, dark and glittering in the dim hall. She breathed in deeply, her breasts brushing against his hard chest.

Anger, excitement, desire, swirled around inside her. She tried to grab onto anger and hold it steady, keep it at the forefront.

She narrowed her eyes and he lowered his hand.

"I didn't want you waking the whole castle," he said, his expression deadly.

"So, you accosted me?" She refused to be intimidated. Refused to let him hear the tremor in her voice. A tremor caused by his nearness, and not so much the scare she'd just had.

"You were sneaking out."

"How did you know?" she asked, fully aware that she sounded petulant and childish and not really caring at all.

"I have an alarm on your door. Silent, of course." One side of his mouth lifted into a grim sort of self-satisfied smile. "Surprise."

"Bastard."

He released his hold on her. "It's entirely possible. Likely, in fact."

"I didn't mean in the literal sense," she said, brushing her hand over her arm, where his hand had burned her through the

fabric of her jacket. "Of having unmarried parents, I mean.
I meant it to mean more that you're a jerk."

He shrugged. "Either way, you're probably correct. Where
were you going?"

"To a drink-fuelled party," she said tightly.

His lips curved into what might have been a smile. "I don't
even almost believe that. Where were you going?"

She looked away from him. "I don't know. Somewhere."

"In the middle of the night. By yourself." His tone was
even, but hard. The control injected into each word more un-
settling than if he'd been shouting. "You might not be under
any current threat, but it seems as though you want to tempt
someone to try something."

"No. That's not it. I…"

"What is it, Eva? You're stubborn for the sake of it?"

"Hardly. I wanted to go out. I'm an adult, it seems like I
ought to have the freedom to—"

"Oh yes, you think you're an adult because you've reached
a certain age, and yet you don't show that you're capable of
making intelligent decisions."

"I see, were you required to pass some sort of test dem-
onstrating competence before you made a decision in your
adult life?"

He moved closer to her and she stepped back, hitting the
wall again. He was so close she could smell him, a faint hint
of soap and skin. Musky and enticing. It felt dangerous to be
so close to him, and she wasn't sure why.

"I've been making my own decisions since I was thirteen,"
he said, his breath fanning over her cheek. "And since then
I've made good decisions and I have made very, very bad decisions. So trust me, I recognize both kinds when I see them,
and I have only seen the bad kind from you."

She swallowed, ignoring the sudden impulse she felt to
draw closer to him. Maybe that's why it felt so dangerous

to be near him. Because controlling herself seemed harder. Because her body didn't quite seem as though it belong to her anymore. "Bad or good, you were still allowed to make the decisions."

"And there are some I would take back tonight if I were able to. You don't ever want to be in that position. Trust me."

She wanted to touch him. To put her hand on his face. To feel the sculpted muscles that she knew lay beneath his crisp dark suit. She curled her hands into fists and pinned them against the wall, forcing herself to deny the impulse.

He looked at her for a moment, the air between them too thick for her to breathe in. Then he turned away, putting his broad back to her.

"Go back to bed," he said.

"You're just…leaving?"

He turned back to her. "Do you need me to come and hold your hand? Tuck you in?"

Her heart slammed into her breastbone. "No."

He inclined his head. "Good night."

She just stood and watched him walk away. And tried not to wonder why she wished he would come back.

Makhail cursed the fact that he felt bad for her. That he felt anything at all. But the look on Eva's face before she'd stormed out of the gardens the day before, and her escape attempt that same night, had done something to him. Had appealed to the small bit of humanity he had left inside of him. One he had thought long snuffed out.

She'd spent the rest of the day yesterday in her room. Her father had considered it a victory. It kept her well out of the spotlight, after all.

Mak had not seen it the same way. He wasn't in the business of dealing with people who didn't want to his services.

And as much as he hated the parallel, he was essentially a babysitter with a gun.

And Eva was unhappy. Desperately so.

I want to live.

That word, *live,* had hit him hard in the chest. There was something about her in that moment that reminded him of Marina. When she'd been vibrant, whole, with her entire life stretching before her.

I don't need anything but you, Mak. Everything else can wait.

Except there had been no future for her, no later time to experience the things she'd longed for. In one moment everything had changed. All of the somedays they'd planned had been lost. And he had thought, so many times, that death would have been sweeter than what Marina had been left with.

There had been many times he'd thought of what he would do differently. If he could turn time back eleven years and redo everything.

He'd been doing nothing but thinking of that since Eva had shut herself in her room.

He stalked down the corridor and into the dining room, where Eva was alone, eating breakfast at the same table she'd eaten at yesterday. A table that could comfortably seat thirty, but seemed only ever to seat her.

"Morning," she said tightly, not looking up.

"Good morning, Eva."

"We did this yesterday," she said. "It didn't go well."

"Not really." He looked at Eva, really looked at her. He could change it for her. He could make sure she felt some sense of freedom. He didn't want to care about her, about her situation. It was a job, only a job. And yet, now that he'd made the connection between Eva and Marina in his mind, it couldn't be shaken.

When he thought of Marina in the same position, asking for a chance to taste life…he wished she had tasted life.

She hadn't. And then the opportunity was stolen.

So much of that was his own fault.

He wouldn't do the same to Eva.

And the attraction you feel has nothing to do with this? He banished the thought. The attraction, such as it was, could mean nothing.

"What do you want, Eva?" he asked, his voice rough, even to his own ears.

She looked at him, her expression wary. "What…what do you mean?"

"I thought about it last night. About what you said."

"Before or after I had my emotional meltdown?"

"Just before," he said. "I cannot change what it is your father expects of you. That's a matter between you and the king. It concerns your country. But we have these months, and I don't have to keep you in the palace. As long as you're willing to cooperate."

"Meaning?" she asked, her tone wary.

"What would it take to make you happy?" he said, his tone hard.

"In this…in this scenario, where you're asking me…I still have to marry the man my father chooses for me?"

"I told you, that's a matter between you, one that has nothing to do with me. But there are things I can arranged if you like. Outings. Shopping. Dinner."

"I…my father says it's too hard to arrange all of the security required to—"

"Your security is my concern. It might have been too hard for the Kyonosian Guard, but it's certainly not too difficult for me."

"You're not kidding?" she asked, her expression guarded.

"No."

"I want…I want to choose my own clothes."

"You don't pick out your club wear?" he asked, one eyebrow raised.

"I…actually no, it's all been provided by the palace stylist. And if you saw what other women wore to those sorts of places, you'd believe me."

"I do," he said. He'd secured the perimeter of more than one of those types of establishments, though he'd never been in one as a guest. It wasn't his scene. Not in the least. "What else?"

"And I want to go out and order my own dinner." She spoke slowly, her words gradually picking up tempo as she went along. "And I want to go to the beach. And…and I want…I don't even know everything I want because for so long all of my decisions have been made for me."

She stood, her breasts rising and falling with each breath. "I… Please don't be lying to me."

"I'm not." Something in his stomach twisted. Hard. "I'm not changing what happens in six months. Just what we do now. And you have to stay with me. At all times. If I lose sight of you for a moment, I will personally lock you in your room for the duration."

Eva swallowed. He was offering her a life line—more than anyone else. Yes, it was just a vapor of what she really wanted. The surface, shallow experiences when there was a deep well of things she craved. But it was something.

Offering her an olive branch, even if he was keeping his distance. It was more than anyone else had done. Her other guards had been silent annoyances, making sure she felt watched, never speaking to her. Never interacting with her.

Mak was the last person on earth she'd expected to break that barrier. But he seemed to understand.

"What's changed?" she asked.

"What do you mean?" He stood and rested his hands palms on the tabletop.

"Something changed between last night and this morning. Last night you told me I was nothing more than a spoiled brat, and I think you were ready to lock me up then."

"It's true." He walked along the opposite side of the table, his fingers resting lightly on the polished wood surface as he did. "It is not my job to approve or disapprove of the decisions your father has made. I'm here to protect you. That's the beginning and end of it. As it is with all of my jobs." He rounded the edge of the table and stood across from her, without the protection of antique furniture between them. "You remind me of someone."

She took a step toward him, an involuntary action. She simply felt drawn to him. Like seeing brilliant art that you had to get closer to. "I do?"

"Yes. She… If I could give her a day at the beach, I would. But I can't. So I will give it to you."

He raised his head, the bleakness in his eyes stunning her, stopping her from moving closer. She wanted to ask, but she didn't. She knew he wouldn't tell her. There was something in his voice, a depth and intensity. There was emotion. It had been absent every other time he'd spoken. But not now. This was something real. Something that stretched to a place she couldn't grasp.

"I…don't know what to say."

"Don't thank me."

"Why?"

"It would be far too close to a civilized interaction between the two of us. It hardly seems right." He looked at her, his eyes assessing. "And anyway, this is all a part of my job. I'm already being paid. I don't require anything more."

He might not think it was more, but it was to her. So much

more. "All right then. I accept." She had to do it quickly, in case he changed his mind.

"Good. When would you like to start?"

"Are you free today?"

"I happen to be charged with keeping an eye on a certain princess today, and I can do that anywhere."

She fought the urge to do something truly juvenile like jump up and down. Or fling her arms around him. "Really. Really, thank you."

"There are rules," he said, his voice hard. "You will stay in my sight at all times. You will not question me. On anything. If I say we need to leave, we leave. If I say you need to get down on the ground and cover your head, you do that. If you fail to do any of these things, I will personally see that you are confined to the inside of the palace, and trust me, neither of us wants that."

His warning glanced off her without impact. She had her eyes on the prize. A day out. The rest didn't matter. "Fine."

"Be ready in an hour."

She smiled and was met with a stony glare in return. "See you in an hour."

CHAPTER FOUR

"WHERE to first, *printzyessa*?"

Eva found herself staring at Makhail's hand as he gripped the gearshift. Light-colored scars marred his skin, tendon and muscle flexing in his forearm as he put the car in Reverse. Strength was evident in each move he made, even the simple act of driving a car.

Fascinating that just the sight of it, the play of flesh over muscle, could make her heart pound faster. The men at the casino hadn't done that. They hadn't done anything for her, not in a physical sense. Being with them offered her a bit of thrill, but it was more related to the fact that she knew she shouldn't be there. Shouldn't be letting them touch her arm or flirt with her.

Makhail didn't flirt. He certainly didn't offer anything illicit. He was simply there. And his mere presence was enough to make her feel so much her body felt too small to accommodate it.

She didn't like it. The annoyance didn't bother her. It was the other stuff, the stuff that made her stomach twist, that was what she didn't like.

"It would be nice to go and have coffee," she said. He didn't respond, only put the car in First and pulled out of the gates of the palace, his eyes fixed on the road ahead. "Then I could go to a couple of boutiques, maybe."

It actually sounded boring to her. If she had some friends to share it with, that would be different. But the only people in her life who really passed as friends were Sidney and Marlo Gianakis. The Greek heiresses were only on the island during the summer months, and even then it wasn't as though they were true friends. Not the sort of friends she'd ever confide anything in.

Their alliance had more to do with a compatible social class than anything else. And since they came with their own security team, their presence gave her the rare chance to get out with permission.

"That will be fun," she said, more to try and convince herself than for his benefit.

"Sounds like no fun to me, but this isn't my party," he said, his tone a study in purposefully undisguised annoyance.

She looked at him out of the corner of her eye, at his hand again. "It won't be so bad." Without thinking, she reached out and trailed her fingers over his knuckles. The contact sent a flash fire through her, igniting at her fingertips and blazing along her veins, molten heat pooling in her stomach.

She turned to look at him. He was still stiff as ever, his eyes fixed ahead. The only sign that she'd touched him was the twitch in his jaw muscle as he tensed.

"Not bad at all," she said softly, letting her fingers linger on his skin. It was such a strange feeling, foreign, exciting.

She blinked and pulled her hand away, brushing the tips of her fingers with her thumb, trying to figure out if they were hot outside, or if all that heat was beneath the surface.

"Why do you still wear your ring?" she asked. In an attempt to get her focus off his hand, she'd drifted to his other hand. And from there to the platinum wedding band that gleamed on his fourth finger.

Again, his reaction was minimal. Tendons flexed in his hand, a muscle rolled in his forearm. "Tell me, Eva, if you were being kidnapped, held at gunpoint, harassed by an obnoxious man in the coffee shop, would that information somehow benefit you?"

"No, but…"

"Then you do not need it."

"I thought we were aiming for civility, Mak," she said, overpronouncing his name.

"Civility, yes. Hand-holding and feeling, sharing, no."

Her fingertips tingled. She knew he wasn't referencing that. She hoped he wasn't. She opened her hand and shook it out. She'd been aiming for flirtatious. Confident. An action befitting the woman the tabloids tried to make people think she was.

The problem was, she didn't feel like any of those things when she was with Mak. He managed to make her feel every inch the spoiled child he thought she was. All of her efforts to carve out some sense of individuality, some semblance of independence, were reduced to rubble with one searing glare from her gun-toting nanny.

"All right. I suppose we can keep all that to a minimum."

"To nothing, would be preferable."

"Well, I'm just curious. And you can't blame me. Of course I'm going to wonder about you. We're spending time together and…"

"Don't think of this as spending time together," he said, his accent thicker than usual, forcing her to listen carefully to each word. She didn't really mind. "Think of it as cars in traffic," he lifted his hand from the wheel and gestured in front of them, at the line of cars that was starting to grow the closer they got to the city. "We're on the same road for a while, but we're not traveling together."

"Right," she said. "Except you and I are in the same car."

They were stopped at a light, and he took his eyes off the

road for the first time since they'd started driving, one dark eyebrow lifted. "You're missing the point."

"No, your metaphor doesn't work because...well, we are traveling together."

"No, it still works as a metaphor. Because it's not meant to be taken literally."

"Well, it's just confusing as we're traveling in the car, but you're asking me to think of this as us in separate cars on the same road."

"Now you're just being obstinate." The corner of his mouth lifted into a smile and he turned his focus back to the road.

A small flutter started in her stomach, growing and spreading to her veins, turning into fizzy bubbles as it flowed through her body. "All right. Maybe a little bit. But it's just that...if we can't talk at all I'm going to be lonely."

"I didn't realize I was meant to protect you, keep you entertained *and* keep you company."

She let out a breath. "You're making it sound like you're nannying me again. And I'm certain my father is paying you enough to do all three of those things."

"Actually, as of yesterday, he is not paying me."

Her mouth fell open. "What?"

"My men made inexcusable errors. And even though I was not personally responsible for those errors, it falls to me to correct it. As I said earlier, it's not about money. It is about reputation, my standing in the eyes of my potential clients. This may surprise you, but I generally aid in the protection of people who are under a much larger threat than you will ever find yourself in."

"Like?" she asked, curiosity too piqued to allow her to be offended.

"Men who dare oppose despots in their rigged elections, people who fight for change and find themselves in danger as a result. Sometimes, my clients are less noble. Sometimes it's simply an entitled sheikh who has offended the wrong people."

"So this really is babysitting for you?"

He grunted. The sound was noncommittal, designed to drive her crazy without him actually having to insult her. Not with actual words anyway.

"Do you intend to walk for a while?" he asked, as they drove through the main street of old-town Thysius.

"That would be good. I could go to the coffee shop and then to a couple of the boutiques. I want boots." She wasn't sure that she really wanted boots, but it was as good a destination as any. Mak, spending time with him, was starting to seem more interesting than boutiques.

"I'll park and follow you from a distance."

She swallowed the rising lump of disappointment she had no business feeling. "And they say romance is dead."

"Romance has nothing to do with this," he said, his voice hardening as he pulled the car, quick and smooth, into a tight parking space against the curb and between two other vehicles.

"I was being facetious."

"Wait," he said, killing the engine and getting out of the car, rounding the back of it. He put on a pair of dark sunglasses. His movements were liquid-smooth, his focus on the area around them. There was no way he could blend in, which meant his only option was to adopt an air of absolute authority. No one would ever question whether he belonged. No one would ever question him, period.

He opened her door and rested his forearm on the top of the car, leaning in. "It's clear. Put your sunglasses on. Let's not draw a crowd."

It was an old trick, and while it wasn't nearly as successful for her as it was for some, it kept people from recognizing her at a distance at least. A person's reaction to her was generally one of calm politeness, mixed with a bit of awe perhaps. Which wasn't ego, it was just her title. She was a princess, and people were generally a little bit awed by royals.

But if a crowd happened to notice her, that was when things could get a little bit on the crazy side. And she wasn't looking for crazy today. A bit of normal, that was the order of things.

Although, she was starting to wonder if normal was possible in Mak's presence.

She slipped her large, round sunglasses up over her nose and took her handbag from its spot on the floor. "Ready."

Mak backed up and moved to the side, allowing her the space she needed to get out of the car. She slid out beneath his arm, his body radiating heat. It was a warm afternoon, a coastal breeze blowing in off the ocean offering the perfect amount of relief from the Aegean sun. Even so, she found she wanted to lean into Mak's body. To seek his warmth.

Denying that feeling before it could intensify, she moved past him quickly, stepping up onto the sidewalk. Mak looked at her, even with his sunglasses shielding his eyes from her she could tell, and she fought the urge to tug her dress down as far as it would go, to cover a bit more of her legs.

At the same time, she fought the urge to flaunt every bit of leg her simple black sheath dress revealed. She wasn't sure where either feeling had come from.

"Just walk on," he said.

"We just got out of the car together, Mak, it's pretty obvious that I'm with you."

"Just walk on," he repeated, his voice firm as he closed the door behind her.

Frustration built in her chest, like a hardening knot. It was completely disproportionate to the situation, but that didn't stop it from getting even worse.

"Fine," she said, turning and heading toward her favorite coffee shop. It had been a long time since she'd been able to go out for coffee. Trips out on the town were a rare treat, typically reserved for the times when Marlo and Sidney were around and their security team joined forces with hers. They were always a spectacle, the three of them, with everyone giving them a wide berth. Often, their security detail would go into shops first and clear them of clientele before they went in.

It was all a bit over the top. And as far from normal as anything she could imagine. This would be a different angle on it. Still, hardly normal with a large, muscular man in a custom black suit stalking her like predator.

She turned and looked at him out of the corner of her eye. He pretended not to notice, choosing to fade into the crowd around him. Not that he could really fade, not in the sense that he could go unnoticed. But he blended into his surroundings like something organic to the cityscape.

He looked more a part of Kyonos than she'd ever felt she was.

She turned away from him and focused on the shops that lined the narrow streets. English and Greek were spoken in Kyonos, and both languages were printed on signs in newer parts of the city, but in old town, it was predominantly Greek. Here there were still market stalls, with fish and fruit and homemade pitas. She liked it better than the polished, uniform look found deeper in the city.

She made her way into the *kafenio*, and she could feel Mak follow her in. She focused on the surroundings instead of turning to look at him. She always enjoyed coming here. It was small, with lavish details carved into darkly stained wood. Old books filled the shelves and mismatched armchairs were placed in front of small boutique tables.

It was intimate. Quirky. Everything the palace was not. Everything she looked for when she sought to escape the confines of her family home.

She approached the counter and spoke in Greek to the woman working the register.

"Coffee. *Metrio,* please." The hair on the back of her neck stood up, a shot of adrenaline spiking in her veins. Mak had gotten closer to her. Strange how she was so certain of that fact. That she was so very aware of him. "And another please. No sugar."

Mak didn't seem like the sugar type.

Eva paid for both drinks and collected the white cups after the woman finished pouring the thick coffees. *"Efharisto,"* Eva said, nodding her head, grateful that the woman seemed oblivious to her identity.

Since the other night's casino debacle had made the news, it was likely her people expected her to be on house arrest. Or at least wearing something much flashier than she'd chosen for the day. In the papers, lately especially, she'd been shown in glittering gowns with bright lipstick. Today, she was much more subdued.

"I got yours," she said to Mak. "We can sit over here."

"I'm not here to be, or look like, your companion," he said, hardly looking her direction.

"Oh, come on, Mak."

"Didn't I tell you not to argue with me?"

"Maybe, I zoned out through half of that speech." If she didn't look so beautiful, the sort of beautiful that tied a man in knots and made him say, and do, things he was sure to regret, he would have slung her over his shoulder and deposited her back in the car. All things considered, it seemed like a good idea, really. And he would have an excuse to touch her.

"You are disobeying direct orders."

Her full lips curved into a smile. "I'm not very good with orders."

"Princess…"

"No one knows I'm here. I'm traveling without an entourage of security which, on sanctioned outings is quite un-usual, if not unheard of. And the barista didn't seem to have a clue who I was. Let's pretend I'm a very forward woman. And I've just bought you a coffee so that you'll come and chat with me for a while. How about that?"

"I have a lot of experience turning those sorts of women down." Mak took the cup of coffee Eva was holding out to him and moved to a table tucked into a corner of the shop.

She was intent on causing a scene and going along with her wishes seemed the best way to keep it from escalating. That was why, in some ways, he preferred protecting someone in a war zone to something like this. In a hostile situation, he would simply pick her up and sling her over his shoulder if he needed to move her.

In public, in a situation where he was protecting her rep-utation more than her safety, it was something that couldn't happen.

He sat in the chair and she put the coffee in front of him. Her full lips tipped upward into a smile. She had sauntered across the coffee shop, each movement speaking of her utter satisfaction with herself. Each step revealing a bit more of her long, golden legs.

She was beautiful, there was no question. He had noticed it the first night, when she'd been putting herself on display, and he noticed it now, when she was practically demure in a dress that recalled old days of sophisticated glamor and elegance.

At least, he imagined that's what a woman might think. Being a man, his focus tended to run toward her toned, tanned thighs.

He tightened his hand into a fist. Not for the first time, he wondered if it was time to find a lover. Well, the answer to the question was yes, it was past time. But there were com-plications. Complications that would only grow.

Eva took her seat across from him, a hint of her feminine

scent drifting to him. Like floral soap and clean skin. His blood started to pump hotter, faster. Thinking of her at the same time he thought of finding a lover was not the best idea.

Another crack in his iron-clad control. She always seemed to be at the center of those breaks. Not something he cared to analyze. That was how he lived his life. He filtered out what he didn't need. Extra information, emotion, and he concentrated on what he did need. Essentials, the ability to act in a crisis. He had to. He had to be able to cut through noise, and confusion, to take swift and decisive action.

He didn't have time to stop and smell the flowers. Whether they were literal flowers or soap that smelled faintly of them.

"Why do you turn them down?" she asked, her head tilting to the side, dark curls spilling over her shoulder like a glossy river.

"You're trying to share again. Why do you go to casinos?"

"We've been over that," she said, looking down into her cup.

"To try and destroy your reputation?"

"In part. I won't lie. But also because I want to have some fun. My father...I love him but he believes very strongly in control and in public opinion. Those two things mean that my life has been micromanaged from the moment I was born. If I ever went on vacation with friends I had to bring an entourage of palace employees. To keep me safe, that's what he's always said. But the reality is it's also to keep me in line. The more I've grown the more I realize that...the more I've hated how much I've always stayed in line."

She lifted her head, and he felt her looking at him. Her dark eyes were still covered by her sunglasses, but he could imagine them, glittering, fringed by thick black lashes, filled with emotion. Yes, she was beautiful.

"You feel things too much, Eva. Take too much personally."

"Now you're giving advice?" she asked, her lips tightening.

"You wanted to talk. I'll talk. Emotion changes constantly. All you really have in life, the only constants, are honor and commitment to upholding that honor. You make choices to do certain things, and you do them. And you can find satisfaction there."

"Sounds noble," she said, taking a sip of her coffee.

"I've never considered myself noble," he said. "But it's how I live."

His eyes were always on the goal. If he said something would be done, he saw it was done. It was why he'd consented to dealing with Eva for the next six months. Completing the task, and doing it exactly as promised, was more important than being comfortable, or happy.

"Are you happy?" she asked.

He clenched his teeth together. "Happiness, in my mind, is one of life's biggest lies. People break so many things in the pursuit of happiness. Contracts, marriages, they destroy other people's lives to find a taste of it, and, yet, it never lasts. There has to be something more enduring that you live for."

She frowned, a slight crease forming between her perfectly shaped brows. "So you think it's more important to consider the greater good than your own feelings?"

"I don't trust feelings. They lead to a great many stupid actions. People would be better off if they used their heads and not their hearts."

"You are a barrel of monkeys, aren't you?" she asked.

A reluctant laugh escaped his lips. "This means I'm…fun?"

"Yeah, but with sarcasm. Meaning you aren't."

"Then why didn't you let me sit across the room from you?" he asked.

"Because this is more interesting. I don't know if it's fun, but it's more interesting."

"And the casino? That's fun?"

She shrugged. "It's different. Carefree."

"And the men?"

She shrugged again. "I don't even remember their names."

His stomach tightened, but not with desire this time. "You find that sort of thing *fun* then?" Jealousy, hot, unreasonable, unfamiliar, surged in his veins. His muscles tightened, every male instinct telling him to act, to follow the emotion, to ignore the cerebral. To make her his. Only his.

He gritted his teeth, searching for his control. Counting on that dead rock in his chest that had encased his heart years ago to come to his rescue.

"What do you assume I did with them? I was in the high-roller room the whole time. They kissed my dice, but nothing else. Anyway, what I do in my private life is my own business." She laughed, the sound strained. "Sorry, that was a bad joke. We both know I have no private life."

A sense of relief flooded him, and he couldn't stop it. Couldn't pretend he felt nothing over her admission. "It's the cost of being royal."

"Right. So tell me, what's in my file, Mak?"

A lot of things. Her attempted escapes, the fact that she was very likely to be matched with Prince Bastian Van Saant. That her grades in math were terrible and her writing and composition were above average. He had a list of things he knew about her, and he'd been content to imagine it meant that he had her pinned down. That he would be prepared to anticipate his charge's every move.

He was starting to wonder if she was right. If he didn't know her at all. She had a way of surprising him as no one else ever did.

"You have no major infractions listed in your file," he said.

"Ah. No major infractions. I would think that encompasses threesomes with random strangers in full view of the public?"

"Yes. I imagine that would bear mentioning."

She raised her cup and offered a sassy half smile. "*I* would take note of it."

"As would a great many people." His heart pounded harder. He had no interest in sharing her, so the specific topic was of no interest to him. But he had interest in her. And his thoughts had turned down streets they should not have.

She made him wish things could be different. Pointless. Futile. Wishing for that always was.

"Anything of interest?" she asked. "Or am I as dull on paper as my life has felt thus far?"

"Not dull," he said. "I liked the bedsheets thing. Shows initiative."

"I'm glad you appreciated it. No one else did."

"I can imagine."

"Is this the part where you defend my father and tell me that I'm being protected for my own good?"

He ignored the constricted feeling in his chest. Or tried to. "No. Because, as I said, this is a job to me. I am not on anyone's side. And, were it not so easy to walk out the front door of my house late at night, when I was in my teens I would have very likely climbed out a window or two myself."

Her left eyebrow arched up above her sunglasses. "You broke rules? I find that hard to believe."

There was no ignoring the kick of emotion that hit him in the gut when she said that. "I did," he said. "And I've broken a hell of a lot more than rules in my life."

CHAPTER FIVE

MAK did keep his distance during the clothes-shopping portion of the trip, loitering near the entrance of a small shop while she tried on, and bought, several pairs of boots. Then, keeping at a distance as she trawled through a designer boutique and picked up a few new dresses.

When she emerged with her hands full of bags, Mak was standing outside the door, ready to take them from her.

"Are you about finished?" he asked.

"I should be."

They wandered back up to the car and deposited her purchases in the trunk. "Are you ready to go back to the palace?"

No. No she wasn't. Just the thought of it made her throat feel as if it was about to close up completely. She felt claustrophobic. Suffocated.

"No. I…can we go down to the beach?"

He took his sunglasses off and swept her up and down with his eyes. "Dressed like that?"

"I want to go. Just for a while."

He nodded once in consent and they left the car in its place, walking down the boulevard to where the sidewalk ended and the sand began.

She bent and pulled her black pumps off, holding them in one hand as she walked down to water, letting the waves touch her toes.

She closed her eyes, heat washing through her, warming her skin but nothing else. She felt cold inside. Maybe it was all a bit dramatic, but she felt like a prisoner in some ways. In terms of what was expected of her, what was going to happen.

She had no idea what her father would do if she outright went against him and refused to marry. So she'd taken the coward's way out. She'd tried to get the men to run away from her.

"Maybe I should just try and swim to freedom," she said, sensing Mak behind her. She turned and looked at him, bubbles of amusement fizzing in her stomach at the sight of him in his black suit jacket, slacks and shiny shoes, standing on the shore.

"It's a long swim to the next island or to mainland."

"True. And anyway, my father would just send a helicopter to bring me back."

"Would he?"

She turned to face him, their eyes clashing, the impact resonating through her body. "Honestly? I don't know. I don't know what he would do if I simply refused to marry the man he selects for me. But I…I don't know that I really want to find out. See, the thing about using my reputation to get them to run from me…well, that way is about them. And I could… blame someone else."

"Easier than doing it yourself."

"Yes. I'm a coward." She looked at his profile. "Soon to be a married coward, I suppose."

"Marriage isn't that bad," he said, his voice rough.

"You don't seem like you'd be a big endorser of the institution. Since you don't believe in love and all."

"I didn't say I didn't believe in it. I said I didn't want it. Love is real, Eva. Very real, and it's not rainbows and blue skies. If you love someone enough, it can cause the kind of pain you can only imagine. The kind of pain you wouldn't wish on an enemy. You think you want love because you've read fairytales. Because you read until the happily ever after. Real life isn't like that. You can't just say, 'This is it, this is the end and it will be all right.' You don't know if it will be."

Eva felt the conviction in his words, felt it cut straight through her. Into her. She had a tendency to roll her eyes at advice, mainly because there was always someone telling her what to do. And half the time, it wasn't so much to help her as it was to try and control her. She'd learned to tune it out.

But she couldn't tune this out. This came from deep inside him. From a place of honesty.

"I...but is it so wrong to want more than a cold union based on...nothing more than political gain?"

Mak turned to her, his eyes searching her face. It felt like a caress. It felt intimate. "It's not wrong. But you don't know if it will be cold. Maybe you will grow to love him, at least in some respects."

"I've met the front runner, and he...I don't feel anything for him. Nothing...I'm not attracted to him."

She was even more aware of that now. More aware of the fact that what she felt for Bastian was lukewarm at best. Mak, being near him, it was unlike anything she'd ever felt. It made her heart beat faster, made her limbs feel weak.

And she didn't even like him.

Well, that wasn't strictly true. At the moment, she almost liked him. More than that, she felt a sort of strange connection with him. She wasn't certain where it came from. What he spoke of came from a place that was well beyond her experience.

"There's more to marriage than sex," he said, his tone flat.

"But it matters," she said, her cheeks heating, her heart pounding in her temples. "In fact, I sort of thought it was one of the things that made marriage worth it."

His expression was unreadable, his black eyes flat, emotionless. But something had changed, even if she couldn't read what it was. The lines of his body had hardened, his posture getting straighter, every muscle tensing. "Are you ready to go back?"

"Yes." No. She wasn't, but she could sense that he was. And, since she could also sense it wasn't because he was simply annoyed with her, it made her care.

She shouldn't care. But she did.

"Bastian is coming tonight." Stavros, her older brother and future king of Kyonos, poured himself a drink and sat in one of the white chairs she had positioned in her living area.

Three weeks after Mak had taken over as her bodyguard and she was completely on edge. His presence, constant, unnerving, had her blood pressure permanently spiked and her stomach perpetually tight. But having Stavros around always helped.

"Is he?" She tried to sound uninterested. Unconcerned. She wanted to vomit.

"I think our father is still hoping you'll fall head over heels in love with him."

"Not happening. We don't have..."

"Chemistry?" he finished when she paused for too long.

"Yes." It went deeper than that, but that was the simplest way of putting it. She wasn't about to start talking love again, not to Stavros. He was quite possibly the only man to rival Mak for cynicism. Or maybe *cynicism* was the wrong word. When it came to his family, Stavros was protective. When it came to other areas of life...his emotions seemed turned off.

"He's a good bet for Kyonos."

"And is that all you'll consider when you take a bride?"

Stavros shrugged one broad shoulder. "It's the most important thing."

"Not…not companionship or…anything?" She wasn't bringing up sex in the presence of her brother.

"It's not my goal to find someone I clash with, but in the end, I'll do what's best."

"For Kyonos, not for yourself," she pressed.

"That's what this life is about, Evangelina."

"That's not how Xander sees it." Any time she mentioned their brother's name, a sickening silence followed. Stavros preferred to pretend their brother was dead, but Eva tried to hold onto the good memories. The ones of Xander smiling, being her partner in crime. Yes, he'd been the heir, fifteen years her senior, but he had made her laugh. Had encouraged her to run across the palace lawn with the wind blowing through her loose hair.

Xander had at least felt like an ally. Stavros seemed to see Mak's perspective as perfectly reasonable. Duty and honor, or death. Jolly good fun.

"I hear you have a new guard," he said. The subject change was another time-honored tradition that came with the mention of Xander's name.

"Oh yes, my nanny. Have you met him?"

Stavros shook his head. "But I imagine I'll see him lurking tonight at the ball? In case you try to make a break for it?"

"You might. But I won't. Make a break for it, I mean." Even if she wanted to. "Will you be meeting possible princesses tonight?"

"No," he said, putting his now-empty glass on the side table. "I'm in the process of hiring someone to handle it for me."

"What?"

"I've found a woman who matches people for a living. I've hired her to go through profiles and help select the most qualified candidates."

"A matchmaker?" she said.

"Not exactly. She's an expert on compatibility and she has excellent connections."

She snorted out a breath. "Only you would turn finding a wife into a job interview."

"It works for finding the right employees. You use a good HR manager. The proper staff for the proper job. Why not for finding a wife?" He stood. "Good to see you, Eva. I'm sure I'll see you again tonight."

"Good to see you too, Stavros."

"Be good. Don't run off." He walked out and closed the door behind him.

She thought about Bastian. About having to dance with him. It wasn't as if he disgusted her or anything, but it was horrible to be in his arms and feel nothing. To have the idea that if she was his wife, and she was in his arms in bed, she would feel more of the same nothing.

Unbidden, her thoughts turned to Mak. To the night in the hall, when he'd pressed her against the wall, his hands strong on her. She'd been so very aware of him, so conscious of his strength, his heat. She'd wanted to lean into him when what she should have wanted was to pull away.

What would it be like to dance with Mak? To have his arms around her?

She shook her head and stood up from the couch. There was no point to thinking things like that. They would never happen.

Anyway, she had a ball to get to, and fantasizing about her bodyguard wasn't going to help her get ready.

It was a good thing Eva was his target. Because there was no other woman in the room as far as he was concerned. Every gown, no matter how bright, every black tux, faded into an indiscernible mass. Unimportant. Inconsequential. There was only Eva.

She was wearing red. A deep, rich satin that crossed at the bodice and flowed away from her body. The neckline was low, revealing the plump, golden curves of her breasts, her glossy brown curls tumbled over one shoulder, full lips painted scarlet to match the gown. She was perfection. She was everything a man could want in a woman, a lover.

His body tightened, need, the sort he had spent a lifetime denying, coursing through him. Every tendon of his body, every muscle, held tight so that he couldn't scoop her up into his arms and kiss the makeup from her sexy mouth. And she was all the way across a crowded ballroom.

If she were to come near him, if she were to touch him, his control, control he had held onto for twenty-nine years, might break beneath the strain of his desire.

He needed release. The kind he had sought in the gym for the past ten years, punishing his body, pushing it to the limit until he was too exhausted to dwell on the needs that went unsatisfied night after night.

He tightened his hands into fists and watched as she was approached by a man. He was tall, Eva only coming up to his shoulder, which put him near Mak's own height. He looked familiar too.

When he leaned down and kissed Eva's hand, recognition hit him. He was Bastian Van Saant, the man who was, in all likelihood, Eva's future husband. Assuming the man didn't find some fatal flaw in her as a choice.

Which would be impossible with her in a gown like that. She was simply flawless tonight.

Van Saant took her into his arms and swept her to the dance floor. Eva's face looked strained as they moved in time to the music, her posture stiff.

Mak moved around the edge of the crowd of people, behind the pillars that bordered the edge of the dance floor, circling to keep tabs on Eva and her suitor. King Stephanos had been concerned that Eva might try to sneak out during the ball. Or to sneak off with someone unsuitable. Though Mak doubted she would do that.

She'd been with men at the casino, but he believed her when she said it hadn't gone farther than having them on her arm. He believed her, because her brown eyes shone with sincerity, transparence. And also because it made him grit his teeth so tightly he feared they might shatter when he thought of the alternative.

Eva turned her head and her brown eyes locked with his. Her mouth opened slightly and the tip of her tongue darted out, sliding across the full surface of her bottom lip. He felt it, felt it hit him hard in the gut, sending a rush of heat down to his groin.

He had no control over his body, not now. A cruel joke.

He'd had nothing but control over himself and his baser urges for more than a decade. He'd had beautiful clients, women he'd been forced into close proximity with before, and he'd never felt the rush of temptation.

The few times he had felt tempted, he'd turned away without so much as a pang of regret.

And those times had been with women who'd been trying to seduce him, women with a lot more experience than Eva had. And yet, he felt on edge now, more than he could remember being since he was a teenager. Since Marina.

He'd managed to cap his passion then, to wait in the interest of doing what was right, and with so much practice at doing it since, he ought to be able to do it now. Eva was under his protection, which meant that the dark, predatory feeling rushing through him had to stop.

What was it about her? Was it her body? Those perfect curves? Or was it the challenge that lit her eyes when she looked at him? Her lightning-quick wit, her misplaced bravado? She certainly wasn't like any other woman he'd ever met.

Eva kept her eyes locked with his as she moved with Bastian. Her petite hand was rested on his shoulder. She flexed her slender fingers and Mak felt a kick in his stomach, as though she'd slid her hands over him.

He leaned against one of the heavy marble columns, never taking his eyes off her. And she kept her focus on him as well. She never looked at her partner. He took a kind of sick satisfaction in that that he had no business feeling. That he was the man who held her focus. That no matter how close Bastian held her, she was not *with* him. Not truly.

The song ended and Eva pulled away from Bastian. She said something to the other man, inclined her head and made her way off the dance floor. She paused for a moment, her eyes sweeping the crowd of people before locking with his again. She inhaled a sharp breath and moved toward the back door of the ballroom. Mak pushed off from the pillar and followed her, ignoring the hot pumping of his blood.

He was doing his job. He was keeping track of her. Nothing more.

She walked out of the room and went left, toward the exit of the castle. Mak wove through the crowd as quickly as possible, making it to the vacant corridor just in time to see Eva slip out the door that led outside.

He followed her, closing the door behind him. The garden was empty, light from the ballroom casting rectangular spots of light onto the grass. Eva was standing at the center of the lawn, just out of reach of the lights, her red dress visible in the dark.

"Where are you running off to?" he asked.

"Nowhere," she said, turning to face him. Her expression, her eyes wide, her lips parted slightly, full and inviting, drew him in closer. "I just needed some air."

"Dancing with Bastian had such a strong effect on you?" he asked, advancing further.

She turned her head, casting her face into shadow, her expression obscured. "No. It had no effect on me. As usual. But it was more disturbing this time since the date of my official engagement is set now. And he's very likely the one I'll be engaged to. If his bid is high enough. I've been too cowardly to ask what the price is on my head, or hand, as the case may be."

"You want to feel attraction for him?"

"I want something. Anything. As it is, he might as well be my brother."

Mak stopped right in front of her, noticed a shimmer in her dark eyes, pale moonlight reflected there, betraying the depth of her emotion. He put his hand on her face. Just to offer comfort, just for a moment. There was no harm in that.

The feel of her smooth skin beneath his palm sent a shock of desire through him. Strong. Foreign. Intense. It was almost enough to simply feel that need. To revel in it, the desire of a man for a woman. Almost.

She closed her eyes and let out a slow breath, the warm air skimming the inside of his wrist.

"Will you dance with me?" she asked.

"What?" He dropped his hand back to his side.

Her eyes fluttered open. "Dance with me. Please."

Without thinking, he put his hand on the indent of her waist. Lust, real, raw, undiluted, shook him. She was soft, warm. She was alive. She took a step toward him, her hand coming to rest on his shoulder now, as he'd imagined in the ballroom.

He clenched his teeth together and took her hand in his, weaving their fingers together as he lifted their arms into position. She pressed her body against his, and he could feel her heart beating hard against his chest.

Touch. Real human touch, had not been a part of his life for so very long. To have a woman active beneath his hands rather than simply passive. Conscious. It was so very different from lifting his wife so that he could change her position in her hospital bed. So different from the experience of changing Marina's clothes for her. Every day, touching her, knowing she still breathed but wasn't really there.

His throat constricted and he pushed the memory aside. Marina was gone now. Truly gone. Not simply in spirit, as she had been since their first day of marriage, but in body now as well.

"I'm not very good at this," he said.

"I'm not either."

For a moment he didn't move. He simply let every nuance of the moment sink into him. The feel of her gown beneath his hand, the heat of her body beneath that. The subtle scent of bougainvillea in the warm evening breeze, mingling with the scent of Eva. Teasing. Tantalizing. The way her hair tumbled over her shoulders, dark, silken curls that begged for his touch.

He closed his eyes and focused on the faint strains of music coming from the ballroom. It was soft, but he could still follow along with it. He took a breath and the first step. They moved in time with the song, or perhaps they didn't. He was too lost in the feeling of her body against his to care. He slid his hand down from her waist to the rounded curve of her hip.

Then suddenly, it wasn't enough. He wanted more. To feel her skin beneath his palm instead of the heavy silken fabric of the dress. To feel the press of her body on his without his suit between them.

Her fingertips moved over his shoulder and he pulled his head back so he could look at her face. Their lips were so close. Kissing her would be the simplest thing in the world. Much easier than keeping his eyes on what he was here to do. Much easier than continuing to cling to his control.

He released his hold on her and stepped away.

"Mak?" There was a questioning note in her voice. "The song isn't finished yet."

"We're through here," he said, his voice rough, his words forced. He turned away from her, his heart raging, his body protesting. "Come, Eva. You need to rejoin the party before your absence is noticed."

"I… Yes. I'm sure I do." She walked past him and headed back into the palace.

Eva sucked in a shaky breath, trying to keep the tears that were forming at bay. She'd thought about what it might be like to dance with Mak earlier. Had imagined what heat she might feel in his arms.

Her imagination had been wrong.

She crossed her arms beneath her breasts, holding herself tight, trying to keep herself from melting into a puddle. Maybe *wrong* wasn't the right word. Maybe she'd underestimated.

Saying that being near Mak generated heat was like comparing a hot stove to molten lava. It was right, but it was far too weak. What Mak made her feel went beyond anything she'd ever imagined.

She burned where he'd touched her, a trail of fire that was sinking through her skin and igniting a trail along her veins, rushing through her body. Leaving an emptiness behind as it faded, devastation.

She didn't understand it. Couldn't fathom how a man who was as cold as stone could make her feel as if she was going to go up in flames.

But Mak wasn't the man she was going to marry. The desire for anything else, no matter how deep, no matter how it made her breath shorten and her stomach tighten, was as impossible as it was forbidden.

Even if it wasn't, he wouldn't want her.

CHAPTER SIX

"You have to get her out of Kyonos. Now." King Stephanos slapped the day's paper down onto the polished surface of his desk.

It had been three days since the ball. Three days since Mak had held Eva in his arms. Every one of those days since had made seeing her a sweet torment that he found he almost enjoyed. To want her as he did, to have the memory of what it felt like to have her heat beneath his hands…it kept him awake at night. Kept his body on edge. Made seeing her and not taking her into his arms again a near impossibility.

And yet, he had not done it. He had not touched her since.

Three days since that dance, more than two weeks since he'd dragged her out of the casino, but that event was now coming back around to bite Eva in a very big way. Or perhaps it was an example of things finally going according to her plans.

"Father…" Eva stepped closer to her father's desk and touched the edge of the paper.

"You have done enough, Evangelina," King Stephanos growled. He turned his focus on Makhail. "How do we solve this?" The king pointed at the offending headline, one that promised an interview with both men who had spent a wild night with Princess Evangelina Drakos before she was dragged out of their private room by her other lover.

"You're right in suggesting she leave Kyonos. She needs to lie low until it all calms down, which it will, once the story is proven false. Easy enough to do, since I imagine I am the man they're attempting to paint as her lover, and the room I took her from was anything but private."

"I didn't do anything with them," Eva said, her voice shaking with anger.

"Don't pretend this isn't the headline you were after," Mak said.

"Not this one specifically!" Eva said.

"You can't control the media," Mak said.

"You made this mess, Evangelina, you can hardly act indignant about it now," Stephanos said. "This is why we have to be careful. This is why I have to hire someone to make sure you're making appropriate decisions. A hint of anything scandalous and the press twists it into the most perverse version they can think of, better if a couple of fame-seekers are involved."

"I have a place," Mak said, his stomach tightening even as he suggested it. "There are very few people who know of its existence. It's completely private. A couple of weeks there should help get her away from the worst of it. You can tell everyone she's gone on a personal spa holiday."

"Good. Take her there. I don't even want to know where it is," Stephanos said.

"Father…"

"No, Eva. We'll talk later. For now, you're going with him. And you will do as he says."

Mak could see Eva tense, could tell she was grinding her teeth together in protest, holding in words she wouldn't say.

"Come on," he said, gesturing to Eva. "We'll go and get your things together."

Eva looked at her father one more time before heading toward the door of his office. Mak let her go through first, then followed her into the corridor. He closed the office door behind them, leaving them alone in the empty hall.

Her stomach lurched. Two weeks. For two weeks they were going to be alone. She and Mak. Just here, in the corridor, with her father in the next room, being alone with Mak made her heart pound faster and her hands shake.

To really be alone with him… She expected to feel a bit of fear at the thought. But the dominant emotion was excitement. A sort of limb-weakening excitement that she'd never experienced before.

She shook her head. There wasn't anything to be excited about. Her name was splashed all over the tabloids, shocking claims attached to it. Blood flooded her face, making it feel hot, prickly, at the thought of what those two men claimed she'd done with them.

"Don't look like that," he said. "You wanted to get out."

"I didn't really want to be barricaded in your secret…. panic house, or whatever it is." She swallowed hard, her heart fluttering.

"It's a chalet. In Switzerland. It's more Ritz Carlton than Alcatraz." She barely smiled, her full lips turned down as they made their way toward her chambers. "What's the problem?"

"I'm embarrassed," she said.

"You are?"

"How would you like it if a couple of women told the world that you'd…scratch that, you're a man. You would probably crow about it. But that's the thing, if I were a man it would be presented as an exploit. Ah yes, very amusing, he's added to his list of conquests. As it is, something that never happened is being portrayed as my great downfall. Sinner that I am."

"We're all sinners," he said.

"True enough," she said, pressing in the code to her rooms and opening the doors. "I know I did some stupid things, but I didn't do *that*. I wouldn't. I have morals." She flicked the lights on in the entryway and continued on through the sitting area and into her bedroom. "I was trying to get myself a bit of a bad reputation, yes, but not…not that bad."

She bent down and pulled out a suitcase and put it on the bed.

"Do you want to call someone to do that?"

"I'll do it myself," she snapped. "I'm not an invalid. I'm not a child. I'm not a slut, either." She pulled clothes out of her large freestanding wardrobe and started shoving them into the suitcase. "I don't…I don't want anyone to think I let those two…"

"No one will think much about it."

"Yes they will, that's why I have to leave."

"Maybe Bastian will think about it and decide not to marry you," he said, watching as she put shoes into the large suitcase. "Or maybe he'll be intrigued and decide it gives him even more reason to marry you."

She paused, her head snapping up, a look of horror crossing her face. "That's…awful."

"We'll go to Switzerland, we'll lay low for a while, and when you come back, it will have blown over. Of course your family representative will give a statement and make sure it's known that this isn't true. But why invite a firestorm when you can go away for a while and wait for it all to die down?"

"What are we going to do for…weeks on end?"

He could think of a few things, things that made his blood run hotter, faster. But he refused to give them voice. Refused even to let them morph into a full-color frame in his mind. The idea of two weeks alone with Eva…it brought playing with fire to mind. Like lighting a match and seeing how close he could get to the flame without burning himself. "Play board games."

She gave him a baleful look. "Scrabble? Could be interesting. We can play in Greek, Russian and English."

The look in her eyes, strong, her wit a bit wicked, even under the circumstances, was unexpected. She truly was an unusual woman. And far too intriguing. Still, he couldn't resist teasing her. An inch closer to the flame. "Italian and French too, if you'd like."

"I don't speak Italian."

"Then perhaps I'll teach you Italian."

"A productive use of time," she said, shutting the lid on her suitcase and trying to push the locks into place. "Help me."

She stepped out of the way and crossed her arms beneath her breasts, her expression imperious. He laughed and moved into position, pushing the lid down with one hand and locking it into place with the other.

"I helped get it started for you," she sniffed.

He turned his head, their faces close for a moment. He stepped back before he could get a hint of her scent. It would be too much. Too hard to overcome the need to lean in and see if her skin tasted as good as it smelled. To get bolder still with the fire he knew could easily rage out of control. "Of course you did," he said, picking the suitcase up from its place on the bed. "Ready for your very luxurious exile?"

"Only as an alternative to Alcatraz."

Mak provided the private jet for the flight. It was a display of wealth that was beyond even her experience. Expansive and plush, with a seating area more suited to a hotel suite than a plane.

It was sort of surreal. And the beginning of real, concrete understanding about who he was. He was successful, she knew that, a billionaire as well, and she'd known that too. But suddenly, out of her father's kingdom, thirty thousand feet above the ocean, she realized that Mak had more money and more power than the Drakos royal family.

Her family had tradition, power and their small island, but

this went well beyond that. When she saw the way Mak's staff treated him, saw the sheer opulence of their surroundings… well, it was clear she'd underestimated him a bit.

Yes, he was doing work for her father, but he wasn't an employee. He wasn't anyone's subordinate.

"Would you like a drink?" he asked, from his position across the cabin.

"Yes, please. Champagne?"

"Of course." He pressed a button on the seat and a steward came from behind the curtain, receiving the order in Russian and going back into the kitchenette area of the plane.

"So, this is your vacation home, then?" she asked.

"Something like that. My place where I go when I don't want to be bothered."

"Makes it sort of ironic that you're bringing me, then," she said, a giggle shaking up the last word. She didn't know why she was laughing, because nothing about this was funny at all.

As far as the story in the news went, she felt humiliated beyond belief. The details in the tabloid were hideous. They'd said she'd done things she'd never even heard of. It was in print for all the world. And people would believe it. There would be nothing she could do to escape that. There would always be some people who thought of her as the princess who'd had sex with two men in a casino. Her claim to fame for the rest of her life.

Her drink arrived and she took it gratefully, lifting it to her lips and savoring the first sip.

"Are you all right?"

She lowered her glass. "Oh, never better. Naturally. I am officially ruined, which is fabulous. And now I'm going to Switzerland to spend some time with a man who really doesn't like me." A man who made her feel as if her skin was too tight for her body, as if she couldn't quite catch her breath. "Fan-bloody-tastic now that you mention it."

"You knew this could happen, Eva. You tempted it."

"I know," she bit out. "I know it. And that's the worst part. I did this to myself, Mak, without really thinking...without understanding what it would mean. There will always be people who look at me and think of this. For the rest of my life. And yes, they lied. And that's not my fault that they chose to do that, but I provided the pictures to go with the headline. I put myself in a bad situation, and I did it knowing full well the press would pick up on it and blow it out of proportion."

"It doesn't matter what people think."

"Easy for you to say. Nobody cares what you do. The press hardly knows you exist, do they? You're like a ghost. I could barely pull you up on an internet search."

"Anonymity is important to my job. I need to be able to blend in."

"Right. Of course." She studied his profile. His straight nose, the strong line of his jaw. Mak was a man who didn't answer to anyone but himself. "It must be so...you must feel so free."

He laughed and leaned back in his chair. "Not entirely."

"My own reaction is confusing me a little bit. If anything is going to make Bastian—and the others waiting in the wings—back out, it's this. And I'm not happy about it."

"No one wants to hear bad things said about them."

"I suppose not. But still, you'd think I could focus on the victory."

He turned his head, his eyes intent on hers, the gray in them as cold as steel. "You're too soft, Eva. You feel too much."

She looked down into her glass and watched the bubbles rise to the surface of the pale liquid. "You've said that to me once before."

"Because it needs saying."

"Do you really care? If I feel too much. If I'm hurt?"

"Yes."

"Why?"

He paused for a moment, his focus out the window. He spoke slowly, as though he was choosing his words with great care. "You remind me of someone. I've said that to you before, too." He paused, looked down at his hands. "You remind me of my wife."

"I didn't think you were married anymore," she said, her stomach getting tight. She wasn't interested in harboring an attraction to a married man, even if neither of them had acted on anything. As long as one dance in a dimly lit garden didn't count as "acting on" something.

"I'm not. My wife is dead." He said the words so matter-of-factly. They sounded so naked in the silence of the cabin. So achingly sad.

"I'm…" Her throat constricted. "I'm sorry." That made her feel foolish. Weak. She'd been complaining to him about getting married, whining about her fate, the headlines. Talking to him about love as though she were some sort of expert and the whole time she'd been talking to a man who had loved and lost.

While she had never truly loved anyone outside of her family. Though she'd had loss there. Tragic loss. Her mother…and then Xander leaving when she'd needed him so badly to stay.

"She was…ill. It was time when it happened. There was nothing more to be done." His tone was flat, devoid of emotion. She could feel it, though, not in his tone, but coming from within. She wasn't sure how, only that she did.

"I…my mother died," she said. "Very suddenly. I don't… really remember her, but I miss her anyway. I don't think it's ever easy."

"No," he said. "It never is. I'm sorry about your mother."

"I'm sorry about your wife. Truly."

"Thank you," he said, in that same monotone as before.

"Will we land soon?" she asked. The subject of his wife was closed, she could feel that radiating from him. He didn't want to go into detail, and she didn't blame him. But she wanted to know. She wanted to help somehow, even if she knew it was impossible.

"Another hour. Hopefully the weather will be clear."

She grimaced. "I don't really like flying all that much. The rough-landing thing doesn't appeal."

"The chalet is up in the mountains. It's very snowy and the winds can get intense. But don't worry, if it's bad we'll circle, or we'll get permission to land at the airport and take a helicopter up later."

"I'm liking the helicopter idea even less."

"I'll put a word in with the one who controls the weather and see what I can do for you."

"Now you really are making me feel silly."

"I'm sorry. For what it's worth, you aren't." He paused. "I would rather fly than drive, but driving is more practical for quick trips."

"You didn't seem to have a problem driving me around Thysius."

"Yes. I do it anyway. But I don't care for it. So I understand."

That simple olive branch made her eyes sting. He was trying to understand her. Trying to make her feel that he cared, even if it was only because he was good at reading people and would rather have her soothed than edgy.

It was still more than she'd come to expect from people.

Stavros was wonderful, but he was distant. He ran a corporation that provided a huge portion of the funding for the national budget of Kyonos. And as hard as he worked, he played just as hard. Which left very little time for the two of them to see each other.

She was also thirteen years his junior, which had always

made her far too young for him to relate to as a peer. Even if things were catching up now. And Xander was gone. His duty abandoned. Off doing whatever he pleased, not sparing a thought to his family. So he didn't do her any good either.

"Thank you," she said. "For that. For…making me feel better."

"That's just the champagne talking."

She laughed. "No, I think it's you."

His expression changed, his face hardening. "Well, don't get used to it. I can't maintain any level of charm for an extended length of time."

"I don't think that's true."

"No, Eva," he said. "It's true. On that you can trust me. I'm not a nice man. The sooner you realize that the better."

His words sent a shiver through her. "You say that. But you should know that I'm a very stubborn woman. I'm not going to believe that simply because you told me it was true."

"You would be better off if you did."

"And I think you'll be better off if I challenge you."

He shook his head and pushed the call button on his chair. "Now I need a drink. It's going to be a long two weeks."

The descent and landing went smoothly. Eva watched as the pristine white ground drew closer, and the plane touched down on the cleared landing strip.

The chalet's property was in an open, shallow bowl on the side of a mountain, peaks rising up on all sides, dusted with evergreens and covered by a heavy layer of snow, smooth and perfect, like fondant on a wedding cake.

An ironic observation since she was so desperate to avoid having a wedding cake made in her honor. Well, that wasn't strictly true. She would be happy to get married if she was in love.

That brought to mind thoughts of Mak's wife. It made her heart squeeze tight.

"Your luggage will have been unloaded and put in the back of the car that's waiting for us," Mak said, standing and making his way to the door as it lowered, and a rush of cold, thin air flooded the cabin.

"Wow," she said, grabbing the wool coat that she'd laid across the couch she was sitting on and shrugging it on as she stood. "Chilly here. Much colder than Kyonos ever gets."

"Have you seen much snow?"

"Not a lot. We've gone on skiing vacations a few times, but nothing recently. I confess, I've never been a huge fan of it."

"Why's that?"

She wrinkled her nose. "Well, it's cold. And then when it melts it's wet. And then you're cold and wet, so I fail to see the appeal."

Mak put on a wool coat, black, like everything else he owned. "I'm used to it. But then, it snows a lot in Russia."

"Of course," she said, stepping out of the plane and descending the stairs, trying to take in the vastness of the scenery. It was all quiet, completely still, the only sound coming from snow sliding off tree limbs in the distance. "Did you play in the snow?"

"Sometimes. I worked from an early age. Not uncommon there. My family didn't have a lot of money so I helped where I could."

"That must have been hard."

"Not at all. It was better. Better to have some control over the situation, over whether or not I got to eat dinner, rather than simply being at the mercy of my circumstances."

"Oh. I didn't...I didn't realize."

"I told you, *printzyessa*, there are other problems to have in life beyond having someone select your spouse for you.

There was compensation. I had a lot of freedom. That didn't always turn out well."

He opened the back door of a black SUV and she slid inside, Mak following and closing the door, shutting out the chill. At least the chill in the air. The chill between them seemed to have come back a bit.

Mak spoke to his driver in German and they started driving along the plowed roads. At least, she hoped they were sufficiently plowed.

"Don't worry," Mak said, "the car is well-equipped for the weather, and Hans will drive safely. It's his job."

"That's right. You don't like cars."

"Not much," he said, his voice tight.

"Is it a short drive?"

"Very, but you don't want to hike up the side of the hill in these conditions, trust me. Your boots, fashionable though they may be, couldn't handle it."

She looked down at her knee-high leather boots, the ones she'd purchased recently. She held her foot up so that the slender heel was clearly visible. "Maybe not."

"No, I think you'd find yourself tobogganing down to the village on your backside."

"Not the best image." She held her breath as the car wound up a road that ran with the shape of the mountain, taking turns that were extreme S-curves. She put her hand on the door handle and looked over at Mak, who was sitting with his posture straight, the only betrayals of his stress in the tightness of his jaw, the clenching of his fist.

It took all of her self-control not to put her hand over his. Not to try and soothe the tension in him. She couldn't touch him. Because, for some reason, whenever she did, it felt as though a small spark popped between them. And if she did it too often, that spark might ignite.

She sucked in a breath and looked out the window.

The view from the side of the road was fabulous, clear, pale skies over glittering snow and deep green trees. But enjoying the view required her to be able to look down over the edge of the road and that was much less fabulous.

The car stopped at two heavy iron gates and Mak pulled out his phone, opening an app and entering his code on the touch screen. "Only myself and the manager of the property knows the code. And on the rare occasions when some of my employees have stayed over during long assignments, I've had the code changed afterwards," he said as the gates swung open. "As I said, this is my place. It's private."

"I get that," she said as they went around another S-curve and the huge log chalet came into view.

It was set into the side of the mountain, the front of it built up on supports, giant triangular windows, mirroring the lines of the roof, overlooking the incredible mountain vista.

The car pulled up in front of the home and Mak opened the door, sliding out and then holding it until she got out behind him. He rounded to the driver's side and spoke to Hans for a moment, before handing the other man a thick roll of cash and stepping away from the vehicle.

Two staff members came out of the house to greet him and, she assumed, to collect their luggage.

Eva followed Mak through the large, square door and into the foyer of the chalet. The ceilings were high, the windows flooding the space with natural light. There was a huge fireplace with a stone hearth and chimney that dominated the center of the room, filling the room with warmth and a homey orange glow.

"I can see why this is your place," Eva said, wandering to the staircase and running her hand over the natural wood railing. "It's special." It said something about Mak that the opulent jet had not. Spoke of his desire, his need, for solitude. Of his enjoyment of a simpler, more stripped-back existence.

"It's quiet," Mak said.

"And you like quiet."

"I do. And you don't."

"I'm thinking of changing my opinion on that after the trouble I got myself into."

"You didn't act without intent, Eva. Stand by it, or abandon it."

The harshness of his words struck her like a blow. The only reason they carried so much weight was because they were true. Even so, the reality of it was crushing.

She looked at the fire, watched the flames snake around the logs. "It went further than I intended it to. I mean I wanted… I wanted. Not this." She'd wanted her father to ask her, just once, what she wanted. That had been nothing more than a foolish fantasy.

"As often happens. People typically don't mean any harm. And those who don't mean to…they're usually the ones who cause the most damage." His tone was rough, heavy. Then he paused, his demeanor changing, his face setting into a smooth granite mask. Unmoving. Unemotional. "Your room is up the stairs."

She bit back a tart reply, something to bring back the moment of reality that had just passed between them. He'd been real there, even if it had been painful. She'd felt connected to him, at least.

Which was a pretty stupid thing to want. They didn't really have anything in common. In point of fact, they wanted very different things since Mak was working for her father, and her father wanted things for her that she didn't want for herself.

But somewhere, somehow, Mak had stopped seeming like the enemy. He felt more like an ally. Although, at the moment, he felt more like a cold stranger than the man she'd danced with in the garden.

The memory suffused her body with heat. Dancing with

Mak, having him hold her so close, had transcended any-thing she'd ever felt before. She'd danced with men before, but it hadn't burned her from the inside out. It hadn't made her feel reckless and shaky, achy with a need she'd only ever felt in the privacy of her own room, late at night, with a fan-tasy lover's hands on her body. A man who could be perfect because she'd created him to be.

But Mak, and the way he made her feel, had been very real.

Mak started up the staircase and Eva followed behind him. Trying, and not succeeding, not to check him out. But he was hot, and his very tempting, muscular rear was right in prime view.

If only she were half as audacious as the news story had made her out to be. That Eva wouldn't blush when she looked at his body, when she thought of having his hands on her skin. No, that Eva would take what she wanted, when she wanted it.

In response, and defiance, to the thought, her cheeks heated.

Mak paused at the end of the hall, in front of closed dou-ble doors. "This is it."

He didn't make a move to open the doors, and she won-dered why. Not because she needed him to open the doors, just because he usually displayed impeccable chivalry, defer-ence to her position as a member of the royal family.

Or maybe it was a matter of the power shift that had hap-pened the moment they'd left Kyonosian soil. She'd certainly felt it. There was no way he was oblivious to it.

She reached out and put her hand on the doorknob. It put her very near Mak and her breath caught in her throat. It was hard to breath with him so close, and even when she did man-age to take in a short burst of air it flooded her with the scent of him. So familiar. So uniquely Mak.

She pushed the handle down and the door opened. "So I'll...go. Can you have my bags brought up?"

He nodded once, his eyes intent on hers, his face still inscrutable. She hated that. Hated that he could remain a complete mystery to her while she had the feeling that, to him, she was an open book. She wondered just how much he read with each glance. If he knew why her cheeks got pink when he was so close. Why she struggled to breathe.

"Of course," he said.

"I'll…" She fought to finish the thought and failed.

"Go?"

"Yes." She stepped into the room, expansive and warm, a lit fireplace similar to the one downstairs on the back wall, across from a large four-poster bed with a plush quilt draped over the foot.

"I'm tired. It's…I'll probably lie down for a while. But if you want to have my…my bags…"

"You want your bags," he said, finishing her thought again. Her stupid, repetitious, rambly thought that was betraying just how scrambled her brain was.

"Yes. That would be…great."

He looked at her for a moment, his expression hardening, a strange glint in his gray eyes. She was tempted to touch his face, then trace the faint scar that ran along his cheek. Tempted to touch the heavy, dark shadow that covered his jaw.

"I'll have them sent up." He turned sharply and walked back down the hall, down the stairs.

She stood in the doorway, watching. She still couldn't breathe.

It was foolishness to bring Eva's suitcases to her. Foolish to desire temptation as he did. To long for that touch of illicit thrill, that siren's call to sin. To invite forbidden fruit to come near his lips, to smell it, allow his mouth water with the desire to have it, with no real intention of taking a taste. It was some new form of masochism he'd discovered since meeting Eva.

He found himself continually chasing it. The jolt of desire he felt when he was near her. The electric rush of blood through his veins, south of his belt, that made him feel alive. Made him feel like a man.

He put one of the large cream-colored suitcases down and knocked on the door to Eva's room.

There was no response, and the silence brought to mind the mental image of Eva rappelling out the second-floor window and dashing through the deep snow in those ridiculous boots of hers.

He pushed the door open and stopped when he saw her, lying flat on her back on the bed, her arm thrown over her face, her dark curls tumbled around her head in a wild, glossy mass. She was still wearing her boots.

There was nothing suggestive about her pose, and yet, she stopped him cold, his heart thundering heavily. The dull throb of arousal working its way through his veins.

Her boots looked like an uncomfortable addition to her nap. Without thinking, he reached out and placed his hand on her leather-covered calf. He swallowed hard, his mouth dry, his body aching instantly at the feel of her warmth beneath his palm. He let his fingertips drift upward, stopping at the edge of the boot.

He pulled his hand back. He had no right to touch her.

Unzipping the boots and pulling them off would be too close to a taste. Much too close.

He curled his hand into a fist and tried to ignore the burning in his chest that was reminding him to breathe. Breathing was a risk. Her scent only pushed the level of temptation up higher, only made it more difficult to stop himself from getting closer, from touching.

She sighed and arched her back, her breasts pushing against her sweater, round and full. He gritted his teeth against the rush of need that flooded him.

She pushed up, her hair spilling over her shoulders. "Mak?"

His name on her lips, her voice thick with sleep, was like a punch straight to his gut.

"I brought your bags. You were tired."

"Yeah." She arched and stretched, her movements smooth, feline. Sexy.

"Feeling better?"

"A little bit." She got off of the bed and walked over to the window, her hips swaying as she walked, his control, already shaky, not up to the task of keeping his gaze from straying to the round curve of her butt. "It's really beautiful here. Maybe I need some quiet. Maybe I need this."

He was starting to think it had been a mistake. He should have found somewhere else. Somewhere busy. Somewhere she might not be as recognizable but could still get out, get to a public place with as many people between them as possible.

Anything was preferable to having her alone in a bedroom, with every freedom, physically, to do just as he pleased.

But that physical freedom, the ability to touch her, kiss her, meant nothing. Not when he was bound by honor, by his word, to protect her as her father wanted her protected.

"Are you hungry?"

"A little."

"I can have my housekeeper make something."

She frowned. "It's easy to forget there are other people here. It feels like we're the only two people on the planet."

"There aren't nearly as many people here as there are in the palace in Kyonos. And my staff don't live on site. They live down in the village at the base of the mountain. I'm not here on a regular basis so I really just need a caretaker most of the time to ensure things don't fall apart."

"How many people are here when you're here?"

"Just Liesel and her husband Jan. She cooks for me, and he does a lot of the general prep for the house. Makes sure the fires are going so that it's warm by the time I arrive. Then they typically leave after dinner."

"So...you end up here alone for a lot of the day?"

"Yes."

A tiny crease marred her brow. "I don't think I've ever really been alone. There's a staff of hundreds at the palace in Kyonos. Discounting the guard, of course. A lot of them live there, someone is always up working."

"So this will be an experience then," he said dryly, turning to leave her room.

"I still won't be alone. I'll be...alone with you," she said.

His stomach tightened. He didn't want to be aware of that. He already was, but having her say it out loud made it even more stark, even harder to ignore. That they would be the only two in the house after Liesel and Jan left for the night felt like too much to manage, at least at the moment. He would get a grip on his control again, but until then, the image was troubling.

"You can't be alone *with* someone," he said.

"Just the two of us then. That feels..." she trailed off, looking away. It didn't help that her thoughts seemed to be straying in the same direction.

He didn't know exactly how innocent Eva was, but he could guess. He had a feeling it was contributing to just how much she was betraying. That he could read her thoughts, that he could guess just what it felt like to her to find herself secluded in a house with him.

Because he felt it too.

He had practice resisting the need for sex. Had it in spades. He doubted there were many men on the planet who hadn't taken vows to the church with as much experience in the matter. Still, she made it seem hard, when for years it had seemed like little more than a mild annoyance.

He'd grown used to it. Blocking it out. And when that became impossible at night when his entire body cried out for release, he was adept at taking care of it alone, quickly, precisely. He'd spent hours in the gym, running along the beach at the home he'd shared with Marina, so that when night came, he could fall into bed and sleep like the dead the moment his head hit the pillow. It had never been enough, but it had been manageable. Until Eva.

"I promise you, *printzyessa*, I will never take advantage of you. I've promised to protect you, I made a promise to your father, and now I make the same promise to you. I will not break that vow." And now that he'd spoken it, it was reinforced. There was no going back on it. Ever.

She looked at him, dark eyes wide, filled with emotion. Filled with everything. They were windows into her, letting him see just how young and open she still was. How unscarred by the things of the world.

How easy it would be to hurt her. To damage all of that sparkle, all of that soft, sweet beauty. He curled his hands into fists, so rough and scarred from living the kind of life Eva couldn't possibly imagine. Touching her would be a cruelty.

"I never thought you would," she said.

"Then you are truly naive," he said, his tone rough, unrecognizable even to himself. He hadn't given himself permission to speak the words, to betray so much. "I'm only a man after all."

She took a step toward him, and he took a step back. "I never took you for anything else," she said. She extended her hand and took another step. This time he didn't move back. He dared her to follow through with what she was starting. He didn't believe she would.

She took another step toward him, resting her hand lightly on his chest, right over his heart. "Just as I thought," she said. "Not a machine at all. You even have a heartbeat."

He put his hand over hers, held it to his chest. He felt as

though he was starving for contact, a connection. For touch. Her touch. His heartbeat sped up beneath their hands and he dropped his hold on her, the realization of crossing a line hitting him a beat too late.

"I never thought you'd do anything to take advantage of me," she said softly, her fingers flexing against his chest. Testing him. Torturing him.

"Then your imagination is sadly lacking," he said.

He could feel his control slipping, feel himself losing hold of everything. Of honor. Of reality. Of everything but the raging desire that was pouring into him.

"You're offended that I imagined you would be honorable?" she asked slipping her hand from beneath his and crossing her arms beneath her breasts, drawing his eyes to them again.

He reached out and wrapped his arm around her waist, pulling her against his body. He lowered his head, stopping with his lips just a breath from hers. "I am not a eunuch."

Her dark eyes widened, plump lips parted. "I never thought you were."

He moved his head closer. He could feel her breath on his mouth, tempting him to take a taste. A shudder moved through his body. Need. Desire. Stronger than he'd ever felt them. His grasp on his control so much more tenuous than it had ever been. Because of Eva. "Then don't assume I'm somehow above the needs of a man. Don't assume that simply because a tiger has been put in a cage, he doesn't want to eat you."

She angled her face, putting their lips even closer, her dark eyes glittering. Challenging. Utterly Eva. "I'm gratified to hear it."

He released her and stepped back. "As it is, I'm currently caged."

She tilted her chin up, her expression defiant. "I'm sure we're both better for it."

"No doubt." He moved to the door, ignoring the rage and need that was coursing through him like a current, ready to overflow the confines of a river bed. "Dinner?"

"I thought you'd never ask. I'm starving."

Eva had never been more grateful to have a large piece of furniture between her and someone else. What had passed between her and Mak upstairs had left her shaking. And wanting more.

She took a sip of her soup and devoted a lot more concentration to watching the spoon as she pulled it away from her lips and set it back down into the bowl. Then she devoted a lot more attention than anyone not cooking the soup needed to devote to the rich red color of the broth. Anything to avoid looking at Mak.

She'd betrayed too much. She'd pushed him too far. Of course, he'd revealed a bit himself, but then…he was a man. A point he'd made very clear. And admitting desire was probably a lot easier, and more common and less meaningful for a man than it was for a woman.

At least, it would be for her brother, who seemed to change mistresses with alarming frequency. Stavros would admit desire for a woman within five minutes of meeting her, and likely have that desire satisfied a couple of hours after that. Discreetly, of course, since Stavros would never do anything to compromise the family name.

She didn't really like thinking of her brother in those terms, but he was the only man she really knew. She had no reason to believe that Mak wasn't the same. Yes, he'd been married, but he was single, and likely had been for a while. Which meant he was probably back to being free and easy with the way he satisfied his body's needs.

And he was also back to that implacable, emotionless calm of his. She'd successfully gotten a growl out of him, but that was about it. He was all hard steel. Immovable. Unshakable. Uncompromising.

"Is dinner to your liking?" he asked.

A bland, ridiculous question all things considered. Did he really feel nothing? Her entire body felt singed and he was just…fine.

How annoying.

"Perfect. Good enough for a tiger to eat, maybe."

He chuckled, low and emotionless, but sexy all the same. "Maybe."

"What is it you do for fun around here? Make snow angels?" she asked, looking up at the high ceiling.

"Not quite. There's a good ski resort nearby, and the village is nice. But I mainly come here to be alone, as I said. To get away from demands."

"Of your work."

He paused for a moment, a flicker of emotion in his eyes. Just for a moment. "Among other things. But mainly work now. Not that I ever truly leave my work behind. It's far too important."

"But you don't generally go out in the field now."

"I haven't been an operative for a long time. I organize, I make connections and head up training. Things have expanded and we now do security on nearly every level you can think of."

"That's…daunting."

"It's how I've made my fortune. Certainly more gratifying than working just as hard for pennies. For just enough to buy food for my family for a couple of days."

Her throat tightened. It was easy to see Mak as super-human. As someone so far beyond her, in life experience, in so many things, that she could forget he'd had struggles. That he'd been through things that were more difficult to bear than anything she'd ever had to endure.

"Did your…couldn't your father work?"

"He did. And we waited in line for food, for the same nothing everyone else got. I did what I could on the side. Hid that bit of extra. There were a lot of mouths to feed. I'm one of five children."

"Do you…do you ever see them now?"

"The ones I could find. I lost touch with them for so long… and I'm not the only one. They all sort of drifted apart."

"How did you lose each other?"

"A number of reasons, I should think. Mostly the pursuit of a better life, which took us all far from where we came from. Though I'm not sure of the specifics for everything." He paused. "I know how I lost track of them, but it's a long story."

"I have time," she said.

"You're trying to hold hands and share again."

She shrugged. "It won't kill you."

"All right. I got married young. I left home."

"And?"

"And that's all," he burst out. "Marina's parents didn't approve, and that meant leaving as soon as we possibly could to avoid her father coming to kill me. Or if not kill, seriously harm or perhaps have me sent to jail for kidnapping or whatever else he might be able to think of. I had gotten work out of the country anyway, which was for the best, for both of us. It was a dream of hers to live in Paris." He pushed out a heavy breath "We were going to live in Paris."

"And?" she pressed.

"And story time is over. You seem like the sort of girl who likes happy endings. This one ends badly." He stood. "Are you finished?"

"What?" She looked down at her half-eaten soup. "Yes."

He picked up her bowl and his and headed into the kitchen.

She watched him go, her mind turning his words over. His wife had died, of course it had ended badly.

But she wished she knew more. Wished she knew what had happened to make him who he was. Wished she could imagine that he'd been happy, just for a while. She hoped he had been. That he'd had a few years of joy with someone he loved.

But since he wouldn't show her emotion, good or bad, she probably wouldn't get to find out.

She tried to imagine him happy, with a real smile on his face, one that filled his eyes.

She couldn't.

CHAPTER SEVEN

Eva settled into the hot tub and let the warm water wash over her limbs. The oval stone basin was set out on the wooden deck, overlooking the snow-capped peaks.

The steam rose, thick and curling in the crisp night air. It would have been relaxing if she wasn't permanently tense from being near Mak.

He made her feel things, want things...

Love, she'd always wanted. And sex, yes, but always the two of them together. Mak made her not care quite so much about the L-word and that frightened her a little. Because she felt that sort of wildness in her she'd been trying to create for the past few months bubbling to the surface when he was around. Real. Out of control.

And that had never been part of her hazy plan.

Everything she'd done had been calculated, and while some of it had backfired, the bits of it she *could* control, she had controlled.

But that was all gone with Mak. Every bit of it.

She lifted her hand out of the water and turned it so it was palm up, watching as steam rose from her skin, feeling the cold start to penetrate the cloak of heat that had enveloped her.

"Enjoying yourself?" Mak was standing in the doorway, all lean, hard angles and exuding more sex appeal than any one person was entitled to.

"Less now," she muttered.

"Excuse me?"

"Yes." She smiled, trying to project a false positivity she didn't feel. "It's a lovely evening. Freezing."

"The trick is to hurry inside when you're done with the tub." He pulled his hand out from behind his back. "And remember your towel." He waved the aforementioned item back and forth.

"Oh. Thank you," she said, slightly embarrassed. Because again, she'd betrayed herself a bit. She was distracted, and she was projecting that distraction. And thanks to her little display earlier, he was well aware that he was a part of the distraction.

"I am supposed to protect you, I imagine letting you get frostbite would negate my other efforts."

Frostbite seemed friendly compared to some of the other trouble she could get into with him. "Possibly. No one would want to marry a princess with blue toes."

"I'm not sure about that."

"Have you heard from my father?" she asked. She didn't really want to know. She'd never seen her father so angry. It wasn't the yelling, because he didn't do much yelling. It was what he didn't say. It was the look in his eyes. That fact that he hadn't quite been able to look at her.

And it made her wonder if even her father believed the story about her. Why not? He didn't know her. Not really. He knew who he wanted her to be, what he wanted her to do, but he didn't really know *her*. If he did, he would know that while she might go out and have drinks with a group of friends, she wasn't going to go and get naked with them all after.

"I talked to him briefly to let him know we'd arrived. He still doesn't know the location, neither does he want to."

She hesitated. "Did he say anything about Bastian?"

"Concerned for the future of that alliance, are you?"

"Not especially. Well, of the possibility of it going forward."

"He didn't mention it."

She blew out a breath. "No. Of course he didn't. Why would I want to know about my future? Insignificant things like who I'm going to marry? I shouldn't concern myself with such trivialities."

"Here you go sounding like a spoiled child again," he said, his tone even, maddeningly calm.

"Really? I must be a spoiled child because I have money, and because I have money, and have always had it, I should be happy, is that it?"

"Money might not buy happiness, Eva, but it buys a hell of a lot of things that keep a person alive. Some might say that brings a bit of happiness."

"So because of other people's problems, people who have less in the way of creature comforts, I'm not allowed to have any problems of my own? This isn't first-world problems here, this isn't me complaining about my flying pony refusing lay golden eggs."

"I didn't say that."

"You imply it. With every word. Every time you call me spoiled," she spat. "Forgive me if simply being thought of as a collectible isn't enough for. I can just see my father making the presentation to my gaggle of suitors: Collect three of the ten most important items in Kyonos and gain a valuable alliance! Pick from the Coat of Arms, the Crown Jewels, the Princess and this lovely settee!"

"Eva…"

"What? I'm spoiled again? To want personhood? To want to have my feelings, my desires at least matter to someone? Damn you, Mak. You're just like the rest of them."

She stood up, her heart pounding hard, angry tears forming in her eyes. He walked over to the hot tub as she got out and held up the towel. She wanted badly to resist the gesture but it was far too cold. He wrapped the thick white fabric around her and held her near him for a moment, his eyes locked with hers.

"I say you're a child because of the way you go about it. If you marched into your father's office and said to him what you just said to me, then I might respect the way you feel."

"Right. Just walk in and tell him. And then what? I don't… I'm afraid of losing that connection with him. What little I have…"

"And you don't think this damaged your connection with him?"

"I'm certain it did. I already told you this wasn't exactly my plan."

"Regardless of your personal *feelings*—" He said the word as if it was an illness of some kind. "—can't you see the benefits your marriage could provide your people? If you marry Bastian, how will your country profit?"

"Military alliances. Trade agreements."

"And you think your personal notion of happiness outweighs that?"

"Is it wrong if I think it does? I didn't ask to be born a princess."

"We don't ask for a lot of what life gives us."

"My feet are cold," she said. "Let me go."

For a moment, he simply looked at her, his grip tightening almost imperceptibly. And she found herself wanting to lean into him, into his heat, into the temptation that his hard body represented. Then he released his hold on her suddenly. She stumbled back and clung to the towel, trying to get control of her breathing, hard to do when each sip of air chilled her lungs. She turned away, walking past him and back into the chalet.

She took the stairs two at a time and stalked down the hall, headed to her room.

"Trust me, Eva. Feelings are overrated."

She turned back sharply. Mak was at the top of the stairs, his face shadowed.

Anger fired through her veins, making her reckless. Or perhaps just heightening her honesty. "Maybe I was wrong. Maybe you are a robot, not a man. You feel nothing. I could never live that way and I would never want to. Maybe if you were *capable* of feeling you would understand."

He stalked toward her, his hands clenched into fists at his sides, his lip curling into a snarl. She backed against the wall and he stopped in front of her, his palm planted above her head. "You think I have no emotions? No desires?" She couldn't answer, the air pulled from her body, deserting her. "You're very, very wrong."

He dipped his head, his lips claiming hers. Hot. Insistent. She sucked in a breath and he took advantage of the action, dipping his tongue into her mouth. She closed her eyes, the sensations shocking her, thrilling her. She could taste his anger, but she could taste his passion too. And she wanted more of it. All of it.

She wrapped her arms around his neck, the towel falling at her feet, and held him closer. His arms came around her waist, his body pressing into her, the wall hard and stable behind her. And thank God for it, or she would have lost her balance completely.

His hands were hot and rough on the bare skin at her waist, his body hotter, harder against hers. She could feel the heavy length of his arousal pressing against her stomach and she arched into it, into him. She'd dreamt of this, of this kind of passion, this kind of need.

But it had been only that. Fantasies with the hazy edge of dreams around them, softening them, holding them at arm's length. There was nothing soft about this. Nothing distant. It was all harsh breathing, heavy heartbeats and uncontrolled groans of pleasure. It wasn't refined. It wasn't civilized.

It was perfect.

He abandoned her mouth and trailed fire down her neck with his lips and tongue, kissing her collarbone, lower, teasing the curve of her breast with his tongue.

She forked her fingers through his hair and held him there. "Yes, Mak. Yes."

He pulled back sharply, his eyes wild, feral and completely uncontrolled. She shouldn't have found satisfaction in it, but she did.

"No." He took a step away from her.

"Mak…"

"No more," he bit out.

"I…I…" She wished she could make her brain connect with her mouth, but sadly, her brain seemed to be on vacation and her mouth couldn't form words on its own. Even if it could, she had no idea what she would have said.

"This cannot happen," he said, his voice harsh. "It will not happen again." He turned and walked away from her and she sagged against the wall, her legs like jelly.

She didn't know how long she stood there, shocked, needy, angry, sad. She wanted to yell at him. She wanted to kiss him again.

"Too bad," she said into the empty hallway.

She wasn't kissing a man who didn't want her.

Except Mak did want her. She was certain of that. But it was possible there were too many things between them for him ever to admit it.

She could follow him. She had almost no doubt that if she did, if she went to him and pressed herself against the hardness of his body, took another kiss, that she could make him give in.

Fighting the temptation to do so almost wasn't worth the effort it took. So much easier, so much more pleasurable to find herself back in Mak's arms.

The only thing that stopped her was wondering what the price would be for Mak. How much it could cost him in honor.

It was the only thing that saw her turning and heading to her room, rather than following Mak into his.

Mak cursed into the emptiness of his office. Every foul word in every language he spoke.

Kissing her had been a mistake.

But it had lit him on fire. He had felt more, in that moment than he'd felt for the past ten years. More desire, more need. More frustration.

Because having Eva was impossible. But she was the one his body wanted. The one he wanted. But his honor was at stake, and it was the only thing he had left in the world. Everything else could be taken, he knew that for a fact.

He'd had it all taken.

But that he'd kept. He intended to continue to hold onto it and he was not going to let one spoiled princess, with curves that were enough to make a grown man weep, challenge that.

He poured himself a glass of whiskey. Better drunk than aroused. That was a mantra he hadn't had to say in a while. He'd mastered his needs too long ago.

Now though, now they seemed to need to be put into place again. And if that didn't work, he would simply deadbolt himself in his room.

The other alternative was finding Eva and taking her into his arms again. Claiming that soft, sweet mouth. Not stopping there. Uncovering every inch of perfect skin. Maybe she was still wearing that bikini. He could release the knots holding it to her body and reveal her breasts. Hold them in his hands. Taste them.

He gritted his teeth against the sharp spike of longing, so intense it was more pain than pleasure. What was it about this woman? Kissing her, wanting her, was an impossibility. Did he hate himself so much that he would choose to want, to need, the one woman who was forbidden to him?

He'd kept control this long. He wasn't going to let Eva strip him of it.

As he lifted his glass to his lips, his hand shaking, he acknowledged, just for a moment, that it was very likely she already had.

"Good morning," he said, when he came into the dining room after an awful night's sleep.

"I hate that," Eva snapped, her coffee mug frozen by her lips.

"Hate what?"

"*Good morning.* You keep saying that to me. I haven't had a good morning since I met you."

"You are good for a man's ego."

She turned her shoulders, angling them away from him. "Find someone else to stroke it, I have a headache."

"You certainly woke up on the wrong side of the bed."

She glared at him and he couldn't suppress the slight feeling of amusement that made him feel. Eva had no pretense. She didn't have the ability to pretend to feel something she didn't. She simply was whatever she felt. She embodied it.

Right now she was anger. It was etched in every line of her petite frame, her brown eyes shooting sparks, her hands curled around her mug like claws.

"I'm glad you find it funny."

"I didn't say I found it funny." He found nothing about her frustration funny. Because nothing about his own was remotely amusing.

"You do though, I can tell."

He sat at the small breakfast table, taking the chair across from her. "Are you upset because I kissed you?" Her eyes narrowed. "Or are you upset because I stopped?" He shouldn't have voiced the last part. It didn't matter. It shouldn't anyway. And yet he found this infuriating princess had burrowed herself beneath his skin, and he wasn't certain how to excise her.

"I told you," she said, "I'm not into ego-stroking this morning."

His stomach tightened. "A good enough answer for me." One his body should not be rejoicing in.

She cleared her throat, her expression comically composed now. "So, what are we going to do today?"

"I thought you'd put in a vote for board games."

"Only if things get desperate." He wondered what constituted desperate. He felt fairly desperate at the moment. Overwhelmed by a need that could never be met, obsessed with a woman he could not have and stuck in the snow with that same woman for the next couple of weeks. *Desperate* about summed it up.

"There's a cable car that runs up the mountain if you're interested. We could take lunch."

"How high does it go?" she asked.

"About a thousand feet. It's a pretty decent trip."

Her eyes widened. "That's…that sounds a bit adventurous."

"Too adventurous for you, Eva?"

He was baiting her. And she would take it, that much he knew. That, and that he was a fool. Putting himself in a cable car with Eva, with no way of escape, was one of the stupidest ideas he'd ever had. And he'd had some stupid ideas in his life.

"No," she said.

Confirmed. She'd taken the challenge. And he was an idiot.

"Good. I have some work to do, operatives to make contact with, but I'll meet you back in the entryway in about three hours."

And by that time, he had to get a rein on his libido. Otherwise he might undo everything he'd spent the past decade trying to rebuild.

Eva tried to keep her stomach from climbing into her throat as the small cable car, powered by a motorized pulley, crawled up the mountain. Snow-capped trees, a river and a small village were growing smaller and smaller with each passing moment. It was like the ascent of a plane in slow motion. With the creak of the pulley system to provide a disturbing sound effect.

The cable car was elegant and warm, designed to cater to those with money and power. She supposed she and Mak qualified as having both. At least, she did, in theory. Actually, her father had the money and the power. She had essentially nothing that was her own.

Disturbing.

Mak was sitting across from her in one of the plush, velvet-covered seats, leaning back, one leg extended in front of him. The extent of his relaxation irritated her.

But then, that was normal. She was edgy, emotional, and he was all calm and cool.

"About last night…" she said, mainly to get a reaction. And she wasn't disappointed.

Every line in his body tightened, his eyes blazing heat for a moment before the flame flickered and died. Before he was able to put a damper on it with that ironclad self-control.

The fact that he had to make an effort helped a little bit.

"It doesn't bear talking about, Eva."

"I think it does," she said.

"You pushed me too far," he said, his voice rough.

"You're attracted to me. You can call it whatever you like, blame me, but the truth is, if you didn't want it, that wouldn't have happened."

He shrugged. "I don't deny it."

Shock slammed into her. "Oh…well…"

"I never said I wasn't attracted to you. I said it wouldn't happen."

"Don't you get tired of denying yourself things that you want?" she asked. She was tired of having the things she wanted denied for her. She hadn't a clue why he seemed to do it voluntarily.

"You have no idea," he said.

"Then tell me."

"I already told you that I don't share. I don't sit and spill my guts to everyone that asks me my life's story."

"I'm not just anyone." Although, maybe she was. Maybe she meant nothing to him. But part of her, a stupidly optimistic part of her, likely the same part who'd thought a rebellion for the benefit of the press was a good idea, was certain she had to be. That she had to matter to him.

"All the more reason to keep it to myself," he said, not denying it. She shouldn't have found satisfaction in that. But she did. "You're my client, or, more to the point, your father is my client. Our relationships is a business association. Making it anything more is senseless." He turned his focus to the view. She tried to do the same, but it offered her no comfort.

"We don't have to *make* it more." Boldness surged through her. "It is more."

"Not to me," he said, his voice flat.

He was lying. That practiced emotionlessness was a put-on, and she knew it now. The calmer he seemed, the more he was hiding. That much she was certain of. She just wasn't entirely sure of what he was hiding.

"My mother died when I was young," she said slowly. "She brought the laughter into our family. She was the one who gave hugs and stayed in my room if I had a nightmare. I don't think I remember my father ever hugging me. Not once.

He couldn't even cry when my mother died. He doesn't do emotion either. He can't even do it for his own kids. Couldn't show it for his own wife."

She swallowed hard. She'd never talked about this, not to anyone. Never to Xander, because Xander had left. Never to Stavros. Because beneath his easy charm he was all practicality and duty. Moving forward and doing what had to be done.

Though she remembered seeing him cry for their mother. He'd shown that much emotion at least. So she hadn't been alone.

"I lost one of the only people who ever really made me feel like I was a person. Like I was more than duty to my country. My mother wanted me to have dreams. She used to talk to me about the things I would do in my life. And somehow, after she died, all of those things died with her. There was no talk of me going to college, of finding what I might be good at. No talk of me finding the man of my dreams, or traveling, or…anything. Some days I want her back so badly I'm afraid my heart will fold in on itself."

She looked at Mak. "You're the first person to really treat me like I matter since she died. And yeah, you do it reluctantly, and you make sure I know sometimes just how reluctant you are, but you at least ask me what I want. No one else does. Ever. So, to me, this is more than business. Sorry."

Mak didn't say anything, his focus on something that went beyond the view, beyond the mountains. Silence stretched between them, the air turning thick despite the elevation.

"Her name was Marina. As I mentioned, I married her without her family's blessing. We ran away together when we were seventeen. I told you, I've made some very bad decisions."

"Was marrying her such a mistake?"

"I think it was. Marina and I were married for two hours

when a man who spilled a hot drink on himself crossed into our lane and hit us head-on."

Eva's stomach dropped, her fingers going numb. "Did… she die then?"

"No," he said. "But sometimes I wonder if it would have been a kindness to her if she had." He leaned forward, elbows rested on his thighs. He looked down, his focus on his hands, tented in front of him.

He didn't speak, he didn't move. His face looked leaner, somehow. Harder.

"What…happened?" Her words put a crack in the silence, but Mak still didn't move.

"She couldn't feel her legs and I…I was fine, I was cut, but nothing more. I'm not sure how that happened. She was talking to me though. And she was rushed to the hospital and taken into surgery. They knew then that the chances of her ever walking weren't good. She told me I wouldn't want a wife who couldn't give me children. Who couldn't do everything a wife should do. And I promised her that I would always be with her." He looked up at her, his gray eyes dull, flat. "I promised."

It seemed too wrong to ask for more information, to make him tell her the rest. But she wanted to know. She wanted so badly to understand him. To know who he was beneath all of that control.

"Then what?" She knew she was pushing. But she needed to. She didn't know why, only that she did.

"Three days after the accident she was being moved from one bed to another. She threw a clot and that caused a major bleed in her brain. It left her with…brain damage. She couldn't speak anymore. Sometimes she was lucid, sometimes not. She would be in pain sometimes…and she couldn't tell anyone. She couldn't even scream. She couldn't tell me. Death would have been kinder."

"How...how long...?"

"Ten years."

"Mak..."

"I'm not telling you this to get sympathy," he said, his voice rough. "If you have any to give, spare it for Marina, not for me. For someone who lost too much, too young."

Eva swallowed hard, trying to keep tears from falling. Trying to keep her composure. "You loved her?"

His eyes never left hers, the lack of emotion, the void there, speaking louder than a cry of pain ever could. "For all of her life."

"Did anyone help you care for her...did...?"

"Her family disowned her the moment she walked out of their house with the intention of marrying me. It was my fault. But that meant I was her family. I swore to take care of her, and I did. In the end that meant having twenty-four-hour nursing care in our home."

"But at first...did you have help? Or were you all alone?"

"I couldn't afford help. I did everything I could to build my business and take care of my wife. She deserved to be cared for. She deserved the best that she could have, to be as comfortable as she could be. I made sure that she was."

She couldn't comprehend it. How a man, a boy really, could endure the loss of so much and come out of it so strong. So successful.

"How did you get started in security?"

"I was always big." he said, a half smile curving his lips. "And I lived in a tough neighborhood. I knew how to take care of myself, how to take care of those around me who were weaker. It seemed like a natural job to apply for. I did good work, so I started helping with more critical clients. I made a name for myself and eventually left the company I worked for to start my own. It's a dangerous job, but if you're willing to take risks, you can work your way into good money very quickly. And that was what Marina needed."

"So everything…everything was for her."

"Everything in my life was about her until then, why should it change after the accident? She was my wife. She sacrificed everything, her family, dreams for her future, to marry me. I could do nothing less for her."

Eva felt that her heart would break. Felt tears stinging her eyes that she knew she couldn't keep from falling. Tears she knew Mak wouldn't cry for himself.

Someone had to.

"Eva." He leaned forward and brushed his thumb over her cheek, wiped a tear away. "Don't. Not for me."

"I can't help it."

"Come here." He tugged her to him, putting her on his lap, his arms around her, hands sliding over her hair.

"I'm supposed to be comforting you."

"You're the one who needs it." He paused for a moment, his arms tightening around her. "It isn't that I don't feel, Eva. I have. I loved a woman very much. I grieved for her in stages. Every time she lost a bit of herself I lost a bit of myself with her. Eventually, I felt so much pain…there was no way to feel more. And now…now everything is just numb." He shifted, his hands warm on her skin. "It's better this way."

She put her hand on his forearm, fingertips drifting over his skin. For the moment, he was allowing this intimacy. Allowing a connection. She didn't know how long it would last. Didn't know why it was happening now. But it was. And she wasn't about to be the one to cut the contact, not when she craved it so much. Not just physically, but emotionally.

She closed her eyes and breathed in the scent of him, surrounding her, comforting her. She hoped he was finding comfort in her, because no matter what he might say or think, he had feelings. Feelings so deep his body protected him from them by hiding the extent of them. By making them numb instead of exposing him to the full trauma.

It was like emotional shock.

But she wondered how much of it was a blessing and how much of it was a curse. She could see why he thought it to be a good thing, and really, who was she to argue? He was the one who had to live with it. The one who'd had to endure watching the woman he loved die by inches over the course of a decade.

It was a pain she couldn't begin to fathom. A pain that really did make her seem petty and childish for complaining about her lot.

She turned her head and pressed a kiss to his cheek, his stubble rough and pleasant beneath her lips. She rested her forehead against him, his body growing stiff beneath hers. Tense.

She put her hand on his face and turned him so that his eyes met hers, his lips so close to her own it would take nothing for her to lean in and taste him. She started to, and he held her away, his eyes intense.

"No."

"Mak…"

He held her steady, his hands on her arms, and removed himself from his seat, depositing her in his place. The tram swung and her heart leap into her throat.

"Would you at least try not to kill us both while you run away from my scary, scary kissing?" she asked, putting her hand on her chest, feeling her heart throb beneath her palm.

When he looked at her, his eyes were blank, his mask firmly in place. "Trust me, *printzyessa*, it's in your best interest for me to stop things."

"Really?" she asked, crossing her arms.

"Yes," he bit out. "You want a kiss, Eva. You want hearts

and rainbows and whatever it is you imagine love to be. You don't want sweaty sex and lust. It's not you."

She swallowed, her throat dry, her stomach tight. She was suddenly very aware of her breasts in a way she couldn't remember ever being before. "Is…is sweaty sex on offer?"

"No," he said.

"Then why bring it up? It's a tease. A cruel one."

He chuckled, dark and humorless. "How do you think I feel?"

"It's impossible to tell. But you don't seem to be that bothered by it either way."

"My emotions might be numb, but I can assure you, my body is not."

"You seem to assume that just because I *am* emotional my physical desire can't be separate. It can be. It is."

"And you desire me?" he asked, his face looking leaner, harder for a moment. More predatory.

The answer wasn't easy, whether she answered honestly or not. She decided to go with honesty, because she really didn't see the point in lying. Not when she'd been the one doing the kissing a moment earlier. "Yes."

He swallowed visibly, his Adam's apple bobbing. He let out a short breath, his top lip curving. "Isn't that interesting."

"I'm not sure if I'm flattered by that."

"You probably shouldn't be."

"Too late. I am." She nodded. "Yes, I've decided that I am."

Mak looked down at Eva, his heart beating so hard he thought it would burst out of his chest. He wondered why he was still being tested like this. Hadn't he passed already? Hadn't he stayed faithful to his wife every moment of their marriage? Hadn't he turned away from every temptation placed in front of him?

And now he was free. His marriage was dissolved by death and he was free to be with a woman if he chose to be.

But he wanted Eva. And she wanted him. And he couldn't touch her. No matter how much he ached for her. It was torture, a new pain, fresh after so many years of blank nothingness in his chest.

But the futility of it...it was enough to make him want to rage at whoever controlled things. At least the things in his life.

"It doesn't matter either way." The words stuck in his throat, but he forced them out. For his own benefit as much as hers. "Nothing can happen between us. You're under my care, you're stuck here with me...it would be unethical."

"I don't care."

"I do," he said. "Anyway, you're bored. You're stuck here with me. Wouldn't you feel the same about any man you were here with?"

She jerked back as though he'd slapped her. "No. But now that I know that's what you think of me, I suppose it's a good thing we aren't going to do...anything."

"Enjoy the view. That's what we're up here for."

She looked out the window for a moment before looking back at him. "I don't like heights."

"Why didn't you say something before we came up here then?"

"Because I appreciated the offer. And I thought I would try it. I'm all about having new experiences. Especially since I have to cram as many as possible into the next six months."

"It isn't as though your life is ending after you get married," he said.

"It feels like it." She blinked rapidly. "Do you know, and I'm sure this is slightly too much information, but here you are, that my underwear is chosen for me? It's true. I mean, yes, I do go shopping in boutiques occasionally, but not often enough to supply my entire wardrobe. For the most part, it's delivered. A whole new set of clothes every season, complete with undergarments. I'm not consulted, they have a stylist handle it all for me. He works off my color wheel, whatever that is. Whatever it means practically, I'm not allowed to wear brown near my face, that much I know."

She leaned forward and tucked a lock of dark hair behind her ear. He had to fight himself, fight every urge in his body, to keep from going to her, to keep from sliding his fingers through the silken strands.

"Anyway, I don't have any freedom now," she said. "I don't imagine it will change when I get married. It'll just be new people ordering my clothes. That's…the thought of that makes me feel sick."

Mak felt his throat tighten, his chest aching, echoing what Eva had just said. "I can't believe I'm about to say this, Eva, but it doesn't matter what underwear you're wearing."

Her dark eyes widened. "Oh, really?"

"No. Because no matter what you wear, you are Evangelina Drakos. There is no one, man, woman or king, who can change that."

She stood, her hands locked in front of her. "But who is that? If I don't know…I can't expect anyone else to care. Maybe that's the problem. Maybe no one has ever really valued me because they didn't know who I was. How can you love someone you don't know?"

Propriety be damned, control too, if only for a moment. He moved to her and cupped her cheek, his eyes locked on hers. "Anyone who hasn't treated you with the care you deserve is a fool, and the problem lies within them. Never with you. Never. You are strong, strong enough to fight against a system you were born into rather than simply accept it. You are beautiful and intelligent, and yes, you've made some mistakes. But haven't we all?"

Her dark eyes glittered. "Do you really see all of that, Mak?"

He moved his thumb along the line of her high cheekbone. "Only a blind man could miss it."

She put her hand over his, her skin soft. He'd been touched more times in the past few days than he could remember being touched in the past ten years. He hadn't realized how much it mattered. How much a touch could soothe, how much warmth it could bring.

"I wish…I wish things were different," she said, her voice a whisper.

In that moment, she was giving him honesty. He could give nothing less. "So do I."

Telling Eva about Marina hadn't been a part of the plan. Of course, a ride in the cable car hadn't been a part of the plan either. Just as confronting her with the fire that was crackling between them hadn't been part of the plan.

Yet it had all happened.

He was good undercover. The man no one questioned. The man who belonged at every event. And he felt naked. Exposed. And he was trapped in the damn tram until they made their way back down the mountain.

Bitterness tore at the edges of those exposed parts of him. Bitterness, not over the past, but the present. That he wanted Eva so badly, with a hunger that made him ache to his bones, and that he couldn't have her, seemed one too many things to ask. He was only a man, and after trying so hard for so long to be more, he was becoming more and more aware of the fact that he was not.

He was human, even if sometimes he felt more like stone.

"I expect you have…calls to make or something when we get back," she said, staying to her side of the car.

"I expect," he said, not bothering to disguise the edge in his voice.

"Mak…"

He let out a breath. "Traditionally, I'm not the one who answers questions. I ask them. My clients don't need to know me. I need to know them."

"And according to you, you can know someone from a file. Do you still think that's true?"

Spoiled. Scandalous. Shallow. He looked at Eva as the descriptions he'd read of her flooded his brain. "No." She was none of those things. Well, she was a fit of two of them, but it only added to her charm.

"Then maybe your methods need shaking up. Anyway, I thought we were through pretending I was only a client?"

He looked at her dark, luminous eyes, the dull flush of rose staining her autumn-gold skin. "Then ask away."

"Would you do it again? Would you marry her again if you could go back and do it all over?"

The question that plagued him. Not because the answer unsettled him, but because the possibility was a joke. It wasn't possible. There was no change to undo a rash decision. No way to stop and turn onto a different road. No way to swerve out of the way of the oncoming car. To avoid one man's brief loss of control.

No way to atone for his own.

"No," he said, the word biting into his throat.

"No?"

"If I could go back, if I had a way of knowing what would happen, I never would have married her. I would never have taken that chance with her life."

"You couldn't have known."

He knew that. But sometimes the weight of the past decade was so crushing he felt as though he would give anything to go back and undo it.

"There was no planning. It was impulsive. Foolish. I gambled with life, but it wasn't mine that I lost."

"You aren't a gambling man, Makhail. I'll bet the only time you ever set foot in a casino was to drag me out of it."

He looked at her, at her sweet, caring smile. So much emotion. So much more than he could ever hope to give back. "Perhaps it wasn't gambling. But I led with my heart, not my head. I'll never do it again."

CHAPTER EIGHT

Eva couldn't sleep. After Mak's revelations in the cable car today, her mind was too filled with thoughts of him. Of what he'd suffered. And not only that, all the things he'd endured, only to come out the other side a man so strong it seemed there was no force on earth that could break him.

She slid open the door that led out to the terrace just outside her room. She flipped a switch and fired up the large, freestanding heaters placed at intervals along the length of the terrace. They brought heat, cast shimmering waves of it that floated across her field of vision, distorting the stars, shining brightly in the deep blue of the sky.

She was used to hearing the crashing of the waves, used to thick, salt-laden air that clung to her throat when she breathed in. Here, it was pure silence, the air thin and cold, drying.

She folded her arms across her chest and looked out at the black expanse of trees.

"What are you doing?"

She turned and saw Mak, standing in the doorway.

"I couldn't sleep," she said. It was honest, anyway.

"So you decided to go outside at night. In this kind of cold?"

"The heaters make it bearable. What are you doing in my room?" She secretly hoped he'd come for her. That he would cross the terrace in an easy stride and pull her into his arms.

That he would bring her in from the cold and blanket her in his heat.

"I heard noise, so I thought I should check. I am here to protect you, after all."

"Valiant of you." The still night air swallowed her words, made them seem muted.

"Don't assign adjectives to me that I don't deserve," he said, his voice rough. "You imagine me to be some sort of white knight, but I assure you, I'm as far from that as they come."

"So you say," she said. "And yet...and yet you cared for Marina. And you won't touch me. You want to, I know you do. But you won't." Her words hung between them, made her feel naked.

He took a step toward her and the moon illuminated his face, revealed the feral glow in his eyes. "But, Eva, I have touched you. Or have you forgotten so easily?"

"I haven't forgotten."

"And in my dreams...in my mind...I have done so much more. Tell me, where is the honor in that?"

"Thoughts and actions aren't the same," she said, her voice trembling, and it had nothing to do with the cold. He was admitting to the thing she'd hoped was true. Admitting to wanting her. As she wanted him.

"Actions begin in our thoughts, Eva."

"So not even your mind belongs to you? Even that you've given over to honor?"

He began to advance on her, his movements sleek and smooth. The movements of a predator. He came near to her, then stopped, turning and pacing in front of her. The tiger in a cage.

Her throat dried.

"I have tried," he said. "But I have not succeeded."

Eva wanted to move to him. To touch him. To close the distance between them, a distance that wasn't just physical. She wanted to wrap her arms around him, to hold him, wanted to so badly her entire being ached with it.

She took a step to him.

"Don't," he ground out. "Not unless you want to find out just what sort of thing a man desires."

She paused, her expression unreadable in the dim light.

Mak knew he should stop talking. That he should never have come out here in the first place. Eva was in no danger and he had never truly believed that she was. But when he'd heard her door open he'd been compelled to go to her. To see her. To take another chance. To test his honor.

He knew deep down he was hoping it would fail. Hoping his control would come to nothing.

"I have thought of you," he said, speaking what he knew he should not. In the hopes of seeing desire in her eyes. In the hopes of knowing she wanted him as he wanted her. "Of touching you. Tasting you. I have thought of you in ways I have thought of no other woman. I was a boy when I married, and I knew lust, knew what it was to want in a very basic way. I did not know what it was to need more than simple satisfaction. To want the taste of a woman on my lips. To want to feel her desire coating my fingers. Do you know how much I want that?" The words came from deep in him, from a place he had denied all of his life. Finally, free rein given to the needs he had so long suppressed.

Eva did not back away. She did not flinch. She simply looked at him, her eyes fixed on his, her lips parted. She did not look frightened. She looked eager. Damn her.

"I would take you," he said. "I would make you mine."

Her breasts rose and fell on a sharp breath. "Take me, then."

Her words stabbed him, a pang of lust assaulting him,

breaking at the bonds of his control, stretching them to their limit.

"I cannot," he said. And he was the one to retreat. To step back.

"Why? Will you be a servant all of your life? Held down by your desire to do what you think is right? What has it ever given back to you, Mak?"

"We are all slaves," he said. "Whether it's to our desires or to a code of honor, we all serve a master, Eva. And a man cannot serve two. I can't serve myself and do what is right."

"Is it so wrong to want me?" she asked.

"Yes," he said, the word bitter to speak. "I have promised to protect you. I gave my word."

"You would show greater loyalty to my father than to me? You won't give any consideration to what I want?"

He shook his head. "I cannot, Eva."

She took a step to him, put her hand on his chest. He caught her wrist and pulled it away, holding her. "Don't," he bit out. "Do not tempt me. No more."

She pulled her hand away. "Good night, Mak."

Regret, as bitter as grief, rolled over him like a wave. "Good night, Eva."

He turned and walked away, out of her room, closing the door behind him. He would go down to the weight room and he would exhaust himself. It was the only option he could live with.

He started to walk down the hall and then paused, closing his eyes against the sudden wave of rage that assaulted him, his hands tightening into fists. God help him but he didn't have the strength to fight anymore.

More than that, he wasn't sure he had the desire to fight any longer.

With any other woman, any other desire, it might have been possible. He had proven it was possible. But Eva was unlike anyone he had ever met, and what she made him feel far surpasses his previous understanding of sexual need.

He warred with himself, a cold sweat beading on his skin. He released a growl and stalked down the hall, heading to the weight room.

He would not break tonight. But tomorrow held no guarantees.

Eva didn't know what she'd expected. She was twenty-one, she wasn't a completely new person. But she'd sort of thought maybe a birthday would bring insight. Far from it, she felt more confused than ever.

Eva rolled over in her big, empty bed and slid out from beneath the covers, padding over to the closet and rummaging around for clothes. She decided on a pair of skinny jeans and a sweater. It wasn't very birthdayish. Normally, there would be a big party with a bunch of people she didn't really know or care about and she would wear a gown.

She snorted as she tugged the sweater over her head. This would probably be an improvement. Another day with Mak.

Or maybe not.

She wasn't entirely certain the moments of unguarded honesty that had taken place between them had been such a great idea, but they had happened. But, something had shifted between them. Something even more profound than the change that had occurred after the kiss.

All that sharing and hand-holding he was so opposed to. And those dark admissions on the terrace. She tried to breathe, but her stomach felt too tight. She shook her head and headed out of her room and down the stairs.

Mak was standing at the base of the staircase. "I was ready to come and check on you," he said. His tone was so much easier than it had been the night before. The darkness in him held back. For now. It was clear he was going with the 'ignore' tactic. Something she found herself comfortable with.

"I am not escaping into the snow, Makhail," she said, using his full name. "I would freeze."

"I know, but it's late enough that I was starting to wonder. And I wasn't looking forward to dragging you back in this kind of cold."

"Even still, I have no doubt that you would."

His lips curved upward. "It seems we understand each other. And after last night, I would not blame you."

So he wouldn't pretend it hadn't happened. She didn't know whether she felt satisfied by that or not. "I'm undamaged by last night."

"I said things I shouldn't have."

She lowered her eyes, looked at his throat. So much easier than meeting his gaze. "We all do that sometimes." She certainly had. She'd all but begged him to sleep with her. The really sad part was, she didn't feel very remorseful about it. She only regretted not getting her way. "What time is it?" She was opting for a subject change. For now.

"Ten-thirty."

"Wow. I didn't know it was that late. I guess I was taking my birthday-girl privileges seriously."

He paused, his dark eyebrows drawn together. "It's your birthday?"

"Yes. I'm twenty-one. I was waiting for a bolt of wisdom to hit me like a thunderclap. With age come those things, I hear. But I feel the same." That was a lie. But it wasn't her birthday that had changed her.

"Happy birthday." The words seemed rusty, as though he wasn't used to saying them.

"Thank you."

"Why didn't you tell me you were having a birthday?"

"I told you when we met that I was nearly twenty-one. I believe you responded with something snarky."

"That sounds like me."

"Yes. It does."

"I would have bought you something."

She shook her head. "I don't care, Mak."

"I do. I'll have Liesel make you a cake."

"It doesn't matter."

"You do."

"I…" Her throat closed up and she couldn't force another word out. Tears stung her eyes. Mak had a way of doing that. He said all the wrong things sometimes. Jerky, rude things. And then sometimes he said things that were so right…things that no one else had ever said to her.

"You will have a cake, so arguing is pointless. Though you may choose what flavor you would like."

"Uh…chocolate."

"Good. And anything else you want…well, I'll try to arrange it."

She imagined that if she asked for him, with a big pink bow tied around his trim waist, she would get a big no. "I don't really need anything."

"But if you could have anything, what would it be?"

Again, excluding Mak with a bow and nothing else on, she thought about it. "Dinner. Dinner here. With pitas and tzatziki and lamb. My mother used to have the cook make that for us. It was something that she liked growing up. Simple, but…"

"Comforting," he said.

Right or wrong, in that moment, Mak knew he could deny her nothing. Giving in to this was far better than giving in to the desire that was coursing through his body. Better, but not easier.

"Exactly," she said, color staining her cheeks. A flush of happiness. She liked being understood. Such simple things seemed to mean so much to her. And he was finding they mattered to him too.

He'd spent so much of his life giving to someone who was passive. He didn't resent it. He gave to Marina because she deserved nothing less. Because, even if some days it taxed him, he desired to give to the woman he loved. But for so long, he'd only been able to ease someone's pain, not offer any sort of pleasure or real happiness.

Guilt stabbed him. Guilt over finding satisfaction in this. Guilt over the gnawing ache that told him how much he'd missed the experience. Guilt over feeling that he was finally experiencing some of the real elements that should be in a relationship.

It wasn't Marina's fault. None of it was.

Everything he'd missed…she'd missed so much more. He had the use of his mind and his body, everything else was simply a perk. And yes, he'd missed out on some perks. But he had his health. He had his life. But there was still a wedding ring on his finger, reminding him, making him feel the weight of his past.

Still, the flush of crimson on Eva's cheeks warmed him in places that had been frozen for years. And he was addicted enough to the feeling to chase it.

"I'm sure I can have dinner arranged. And until then?"

"I don't know."

Curiosity, curiosity that went beyond what he'd read in her file, prickled his scalp. "What do you normally do in a day?"

She half shrugged, her eyes straying around the room. "I…I read a lot. I go to approved functions. Sometimes— rarely—I go down into the city and get coffee, go to the bookstore. But all of that is such a big deal that I really don't do if very often. When I was in school, that filled up a lot of my time. I finished high school early and moved on to college courses, but I did all of that with tutors at the palace and now…there seem to be too many hours in the day sometimes. And other times nowhere near enough. I can't even imagine the frenzy of a wedding…"

Her sentence trailed off, her expression turning serious. "And when Stavros gets married, well, that will be an even bigger deal. Because he'll be marrying the future queen of Kyonos."

"You'll be the future queen of a country as well. Of Bastian's country most likely."

Eva looked down at her hands. "I suppose so. I hadn't put a lot of thought into it."

"No? Most people would. Most people would be counting the days until the upgrade."

"You already know I'm not. Why would I have any more power as queen than I have now? I'll be part of Bastian's decor rather than my father's."

"You'll be more than that," he said, trying to erase the bleak picture her words painted.

"Right. I'll also be expected to sleep with him. And have his children. Assuming, of course, he still wants me."

"No word yet?" He did his best to blot out the image of Eva in bed with a man, his strong hands on her round, shapely hips. It was far too easy to imagine they were his own hands, gripping her soft flesh as he thrust into her body.

The thought of it made all of the moisture in his throat turn to dust. Last night had shown him just how close he was to breaking free of his control. Allowing anything that remotely resembled a fantasy today would be far too dangerous.

"No," she said tightly. "When I hear, I assure you, you'll be the first to know. Mainly because there's no one else here."

"I am honored, *printzyessa*," he said, taking a step away from her. Distance was a necessity.

"Somehow, I doubt that."

He wanted to touch her, to offer some sort of comfort. But

his intentions would be far from honorable. He did want to offer comfort of some kind, but more than that, he just wanted to feel her skin beneath his hands. To touch the flame, quickly, to see if he could do it without getting burned.

But if he did, it would not stop at his fingertips brushing her cheek, or his lips brushing hers. No. If he touched her again…he would not be able to stop.

Which made the distance even more important.

"I have some calls to catch up on." It was true. There were always calls to make. But the urgency had more to do with her than anything else.

"Okay," she said.

"I'll see you tonight."

"Okay," she said again.

"Did you want…something else?" he asked, trying to figure out her mood. Trying and failing.

"No. I said I was fine. I'll see you at dinner."

She wanted him to stay, that much he knew. But if he did… right now if he stayed he wasn't certain he could trust the strength of his control. For the first time in his life, he wasn't sure if his honor was stronger than his desire.

It was probably stupid to dress up for dinner, but it was her birthday. Although, rather than the customary glittery ball gown she opted for something more subdued. Shorter. Clingier. A little sexier…

Even if it didn't change anything, she liked it when Mak looked at her as though she was a delicacy, rare and tempting. No matter how big a tease it was, she felt compelled to chase the feeling. Even if there was no hope of anything ever coming from it.

It felt good to be wanted.

It was more than that though. Bastian was attracted to her. She saw it in his eyes, felt it in the tension of his body every time they danced. The men she'd been with at the casino had been attracted to her too.

And while all of those men were decently good-looking, they didn't heat her blood the way Mak did. They didn't make her feel. Mak made her aware of all kinds of things she'd never been aware of before meeting him. Both physically and emotionally.

She'd never felt someone else's pain before meeting him. Had never wanted so badly to heal someone else's hurts. If she was honest, she'd always been self-centered. Her life was conducive to it. Her family didn't have a lot of time for her, her mother was gone, her friends were seasonal.

That left her with staff mainly, and as long as whims didn't extend beyond the palace walls, they were met. She had a lot of time to focus on her own needs, her own wants. Much more time than she'd spent focusing on the needs of others.

But Mak tore her focus outward. All of her feelings felt extracted from her, laid out, bare and raw, just for him.

It scared her. And it made her feel alive.

She walked into the kitchen and her stomach did a free fall when she saw Mak standing in front of the stove, cutting cooked lamb into thin strips.

"You're cooking?"

He shrugged. "Liesel did most of it. I'm just doing the finishing touches so she and Jan could get down the mountain before dark."

"That was…nice of you."

He looked more approachable in a tight black T-shirt, and dark jeans. His feet were bare, which seemed…intimate somehow. Something about his more-relaxed self made her even more nervous. Maybe because it amped her attraction up even more.

Something she hadn't realized was possible.

"You're so surprised that I can cut my own meat? I can

cook, you know. I spend a lot of time preparing my own meals."

It seemed as though he wanted to say more, but he stopped himself.

"What?" she asked.

"What?" he countered, taking the platter from the counter, laden with lamb and pita bread, a small bowl of tzatziki in the center.

"You wanted to say more."

He shrugged, the corners of his mouth tugging down. "It's your birthday."

"So. That doesn't mean you can't tell me something." He walked out of the kitchen, heading to the dining room. She followed him. "In fact, I think that's what I want."

"What do you want?" he asked, setting the platter on the large wooden dining table that was positioned next to floor-to-ceiling windows, making the most of the view. The setting sun threw bits of pink glitter onto the snow, creating the impression of shimmering heat on ice.

"For you to tell me something. Anything. Just...don't be so careful about what you say all the time. Talk to me. I like it when we talk."

"Dangerous things get said when you and I talk," he said, rounding the table to where she was standing and pulling a chair out. He inclined his head. "Have a seat."

"I'm..." She sat and he pushed her chair in. She couldn't deny the truth in that. "Well, we could always talk about those other things. We could talk about last night..."

"Never mind. I used to cook for myself. A lot. That's what I was going to say." He sat down in the seat across from her and picked up a bowl that had already been sitting on the table, serving her a green salad before offering her bread and lamb.

"Oh." She picked up her fork and let it hover above her salad. "I guess I just thought...you have a housekeeper."

He nodded. "Now. I didn't always. I worked, I cared for Marina, I made sure we both ate. But I started getting offered those high-profile jobs that were matters of international security, and with that came more money. And less time at home. So eventually I had people sharing care, household chores. In the end, I hardly even had to be home. So, I hope you're not imagining me as a saint. I'm a pretty selfish bastard, it turns out. Sometimes I would come here to the chalet so I didn't have to go home in between jobs."

"That doesn't make you selfish, Mak. You cared for her as best as you could, but it's not like she was really your wife."

"That's where you're wrong. She was my wife. In sickness and in health, yes? Or does it only mean sickness to a certain point?"

"I…no."

"Forsaking all others, as long as we both shall live," he said.

Eva's heart crumpled, as though Mak had taken it and squeezed it tight in his fist. "You really did?"

"I made vows to Marina. I kept them. We were married for over ten years."

Eva set her fork down. "But…"

"Now I've talked. How was your birthday?"

"Fine. But, Mak…"

"Was there something confusing about what I just said?" he bit out.

"I…" Yes. Everything about it was confusing. Her brother changed mistresses with frequency, albeit discreetly, and her father had always done the same. She'd always imagined he'd done it even when her mother had been alive, though in his way, he'd loved her mother. To hear that Mak had stayed faithful to his wife for ten years, when there was no way they could have made love…it was beyond anything she'd been shown was possible. "No. Nothing."

"Good. What did you do today?"

"I read. Went in the hot tub again. Drank hot chocolate and looked out the window. It was very nice."

"That's good. Do you usually have a party?"

"Yes. But I don't know if it really feels like it's for me. And here I go again whining about my problems, which include opulent balls now. I have been selfish in some ways, Mak. I see that now."

He shook his head. "I don't think you have been. Everyone, no matter where they come from, wants someone to care for them based on who they are."

"Except for you," she said, gently.

"Well, I've had it. And it can be wonderful. And then when you lose it, you're very conscious of how great a loss it is."

"That I do understand. My mother…she cared about me. About us. So very much. I got the feeling that there was nothing I could do that would make her see me as anything less than perfect. With my father, it's sort of the opposite problem."

"I'm sure he loves you."

"Like Marina's family loved her?"

His expression hardened. "I was foolish. I asked her to go against their wishes."

"But shouldn't real family just want you to be happy? You're a good man, Mak. Why didn't they want her to marry you?"

"We were young. Too young. They were thought it would ruin her life. It turned out they weren't far from the truth."

"Because you were in an accident? It could have happened any time, anywhere. And then you cared for her. You've given up so much, and you did it for her. Her family doesn't convince me that love is real, or that it's anything I might want. But you do. To be loved the way you loved her…" her throat closed up, emotion coursing through her. "Well, anyone would be lucky to experience that."

His eyes met hers, and she was stunned by the depth of emotion there. Usually he kept everything veiled, concealed, and now, in this moment, the veil was torn and she could see a depth, a pain, that went so deep she had no idea how he could ever climb out of it. How anyone could.

Mak was the strongest man she'd ever met, and it had nothing to do with the strength of his body.

"Love is overrated," he said.

Though they both knew it wasn't. Because Mak himself embodied how much love was worth. Real love. He'd demonstrated it to his wife daily. And he was changing how Eva saw it too.

Eva stood up, her body trembling. She needed to touch him, needed to show him evidence of the emotion, the need that had her in its grip. She just wasn't certain how. Or where it would lead. But she needed to take the chance.

She rounded the table and went to stand in front of him. He only looked at her, immobile, eyes unreadable. She leaned in, hands shaking as she placed her palms flat on his cheeks, moving her fingertips over his skin.

The air between them felt tight, as if it was closing in around them. There was no sound, only their breathing, harsh, uneven. Mak raised his eyes and caught her gaze, his brows locked together, his jaw set tight, a muscle in his face ticking. He was waiting. Waiting to see what she would do.

So was she.

She slid her thumb over his bottom lip. He tasted her, the tip of his tongue hot and slick on her skin. A tremor shot through her, an arrow of desire that made her core ache, her breasts feel heavy.

She started to lean in and he put his hand over hers, pinning it to the table. "Think this through before you do any-thing," he said, his words strangled.

"I have," she said. "You aren't the only one who wants things, Mak. I want to touch you. To see you. Everywhere."

"Eva," her name was like a prayer on his lips. Or a curse. She wasn't certain.

"Let me," she said.

Desire made her bold. It made her certain. She didn't ques-tion what she wanted, not now. She knew. She bent down and kissed him, his lips firm beneath hers.

He didn't move, he simply let her explore his mouth, trace the outline of his lips with her tongue. A shudder moved through his body as his hands came up to grip her hips. His fingers were tight on her hips, fingers digging into her flesh.

She broke the kiss, rested her forehead against his. "I've never done that before," she whispered, each word broken by a shaky breath.

"You do it very well," he said, his voice rough.

"Hmm," She leaned in and kissed his mouth again, softly. "I'm glad you like it."

He swallowed, his Adam's apple dipping. "Too much."

She slid her fingers through his hair, and he kept his hands firmly planted on her hips, his eyes never leaving hers. "What's wrong with liking it?" she asked.

He chuckled, that same sort of bitter, humorless release she'd become accustomed to hearing from him. "We've been over this before, my princess. I am meant to protect you. This isn't protecting you." His tone was bogged down with weight. With regret.

"But I want it."

"You imagine I don't?"

"You asked me what I wanted for my birthday, and I was honest. Dinner was lovely. But I left out a big part of what I wanted. I want you, Mak. I want to…to be with you."

He turned his head away. "Why?"

She pushed his hair off his forehead, the gesture natural and thrilling at the same time. "Because I want you. Isn't that enough?"

He turned to face her again, his expression so hungry it was almost frightening. Almost. "Want is…want is something I've spent a very long time ignoring. Want is something I've spent a very long time pretending doesn't matter. There has only been necessity. Only breathing."

"I've never had a chance to let it matter. So now, maybe we can both have it. Even if it's just for a while." She choked on a sob. "Please don't make me marry a man I don't want without ever knowing what it's like to be with one I do want. And before you say anything, it's you I want. Not just the experience. I could have had both of those men at the casino. A half a dozen others before them if I'd been motivated to pursue them. I didn't. But you, you're worth me…putting myself out here like this. I'm risking a lot here. But it's worth it."

His fingers curled against her hips as he tightened his hands into fists, still holding her near him. He closed his eyes and looked away, pain, need, etched into every line of his face. "I have done all that I could do to be an honorable man. To honor my wife. To stay true to my vows. And still, even since her death, I have not taken a lover. And you are the last woman that I should want. But God help me I want you." It was prayer more than it was a curse. As though he was truly appealing for help from a higher power.

He took a sharp breath. "I desire you so much that my body shakes when I think of you. I have denied myself, denied my desires, for so long and you…you make me wish I didn't care. That I didn't have to choose between right and want." He looked up at her, his eyes blazing with heat. "For the first time, I choose want. And I want you, Princess Evangelina Drakos."

CHAPTER NINE

"Be sure," he said, watching her eyes, trying to get a read on her thoughts. "Because if this starts…" He wouldn't be able to stop. Although, admitting that out loud was close to torture.

He prided himself on his control. And his control was iron. He'd proven it on more than one occasion. But he was about to let it go now. To release his hold on it completely. And once he did that, he wasn't certain how long it would take for him to grasp it again.

He'd spent his life clinging to it. Trying to do the right thing by Marina, to marry her before consummating their relationship. Waiting longer, while he cared for a wife. While he turned down the advances of every woman who gave him a coy look or an overt invitation.

Waiting still because he really hadn't figured out how to rejoin the world of the living. Not after so many years.

And now, now his limit had been reached. A beast inside him had been unleashed.

It was easy to imagine it was because he had allowed it to be set free. But he knew it was truly because of Eva. Because she appealed to something in him that went beyond simple arousal. She was like him in so many ways, bound by circumstances she couldn't control.

But she fought against them. She fought with power, with wit. Bravery. She didn't think twice about challenging him.

About seducing him, even though he was certain she was a virgin.

She had fire in her. And he only had cold stone. Just for a while, for a moment, he wanted to be warm. To be with her.

"I'm sure," she said. She lowered herself onto his lap and he put his hands on her waist. She dipped her head to kiss him.

"Wait," he said, his throat tight. She looked shocked, but froze in place. "I just want to look at you for a moment. To know that tonight, you'll be mine." He moved his hands through her thick, dark hair, finally able to relish the feel of the silken curls.

Guilt had no place in things tonight. Tomorrow, it would be there. It always was. Guilt was his constant companion, gnawing at him always, the reasons varied, but ever-present.

Not tonight.

Tonight there was only Eva. Only his desire for her. Needs that would finally be met.

Her lip trembled and he leaned forward and kissed her lightly. Eva melted into him, her breasts pressing against his chest, her curves melding to him as she gave herself over to the kiss. And he allowed himself to relish it. Her tongue, smooth and hot, her lips so soft and sweet, perfect.

He was dying to touch her. To explore those soft, feminine curves, so different from his own body. This was what he was made for, a part of himself he had denied for so long. He reached behind her and took the zipper on her dress between his thumb and forefinger, sliding it down slowly, savoring the action. Savoring the experience of undressing a woman who was so alive. So responsive.

It was a beautiful dress, one that had kicked his libido into high gear the moment she'd come down for dinner. But it wasn't enough. He wanted more. All of her, without any fabric covering her luscious golden skin. Without anything between them at all.

He tugged the top of her dress down slowly, revealing more of her rounded breasts with each shift of fabric. His breath stopped completely when the top fell down around her stomach and revealed a thin black lace bra that showed hints of erect, caramel-colored nipples beneath the flimsy fabric.

He lowered his head and kissed the curve of one breast, a sharp shock of need piercing him in the gut, making his erection pulse.

Arousal stabbed him, hot and fierce, a rush of desire overwhelming him for a moment. He closed his eyes and gritted his teeth. Yes, he was letting go of his control. And yes, in many ways, this night was for him.

But it was hers too. And he would be damned if it was anything less than perfect for Eva. If she was anything less than satisfied.

"You are incredible," he rasped, raising his head so that he could look at her face. She was exquisitely beautiful. High cheekbones, a strong, rounded nose, full lips. There was nothing generic about her, nothing forgettable. She would be burned into his mind, his body, forever.

"I'll bet you say that to all the women," she said.

He felt his muscles tense, his fingers curling into her back. There was no easy way to have the conversation they would have to have tonight. But she was owed his honesty. She was giving him her body, and she deserved to know.

This was the conversation he'd never wanted to have. And yet, somehow, with Eva, it didn't seem so impossible.

"There have been no other women." He watched her face, waiting for his words to sink in, for her to understand. Waiting to see if she would be horrified. If she would want to stop.

Her dark eyes widened. "That's not possible."

"It is. When you're married for over ten years to a wife who is incapable. And when you refuse to violate your marriage vows, no matter what."

"And for the past year?"

"I haven't been ready to seek anyone out. I haven't wanted anyone." He touched her face, traced the line of her brow, her nose, her lips. "Until you."

Her dark eyes glistened, a tear spilling over and dropping down her cheek, landing on his hand. "Why?"

"You're the only woman who's ever made me feel like I didn't want to be controlled anymore," he said, the words not coming easily. "You are…fire, Eva. So hot beneath my hands. Lust I can deny, I have, for years. This is more than that. But I understand if you don't want to be with me now."

"Why?" she breathed. "Why would I not want you?"

"I'm not a playboy. Not a man who can give you the benefit of much practiced skill." He tucked a stray lock of hair behind her ear. "Most would see it as a weakness."

"Then most people are foolish. It takes strength to do what you've done. Any man could have stayed with his wife while continuing to live his own life. While continuing to make sure his wife's needs were met. What you've done…you made a choice. A hard choice. You kept your commitments. I didn't think it was possible, but I want you even more now."

He let out a breath. "A relief, for sure."

She leaned in and kissed his cheek. "I think you are the best man I've ever known. A real man."

"I'll confess, I lack hands-on experience. However, I can dismantle a bomb in under sixty seconds. That requires skill, dexterity, concentration. I'm sure I can apply it."

She laughed and his heart missed a beat. "I never doubted you for a moment."

He lowered his head again, tracing the line where lace met flesh, just above her nipple. A short, muffled sound of pleasure escaped Eva's lips and he reveled in the response.

He reached around and unhooked her bra, finally seeing

her uncovered for the first time. He'd seen naked women. He'd seen Marina's body many times while taking care of her.

This was different. Different than a photograph or movie. Different than a woman walking by on a topless beach. Different than caring for someone whose body was present, but who no longer had her mind.

"More beautiful than I ever could have imagined," he said, cupping her flesh in his hands, brushing her taut nipples with his thumbs. She let her head fall back, and she didn't bother to contain the her exclamation of pleasure this time.

He kept his eyes locked with hers as he dipped his head and circled one tightened bud with the tip of his tongue. Her body shuddered over his, and it echoed through him, reverberating along every line, every muscle, creating a deep, pulling pleasure in his groin.

He sucked harder in response and she gasped, her fingers digging into his shoulders. He raised his head. "Good?"

"Yes. Good....good doesn't describe it."

Then he scooped her up in his arms and she looped hers around his neck, delicate fingers moving through his hair as he walked from the dining room to the living area and up the stairs.

"This is like a movie," she said. "Only I doubt it will fade to black at the important part."

"It better not," he said, opening the door to her room and setting her on the bed.

He put his knee down on the soft mattress and bent to kiss her, she arched against him, returning the kiss eagerly, her tongue soft and slick against his.

Just the thought of where it would lead, of how it would feel to have her soft, bare body pressed against his, of what it would be like to slide into her tight, wet heat, made him shake.

As the image entered his mind, so did another concern. He swore.

"What?" she asked.

"Protection. I haven't got any, for obvious reasons."

"I…I saw some," she said, her voice small.

"You did?"

"In my bathroom."

It took him a moment to remember he'd let Jiminez, one of the most trusted men on his staff, stay in the chalet last summer when he'd had some heat put on him by opposing factions. He hadn't given him permission to bring a woman, but he'd never been so grateful for someone to breach protocol in his life. "One of my operatives," he said.

"I believe what you said to me," she said. "If I didn't…" she looked up at the ceiling, then around. "Well, if I didn't we shouldn't be here. This might be temporary, but…we do have a connection. At least I feel one with you."

In all honesty, he couldn't remember the last time he'd felt connected with anything. Anything beyond vague, cold concepts of honor, of right and wrong. He'd cut off the flow to his heart and dwelt in his head.

But Eva forced him back to his body, back to feelings and passion and desire. Caring. Things he'd been certain he'd lost.

"This is beyond my experience," he said, knowing he owed her honesty. No empty promises. "And you are the most amazing woman."

She smiled faintly. "You say the nicest things."

Nice. He'd never been accused of being nice. "I'll get the condoms."

Eva was there, waiting for him, her mouth curved up, resting on the pillows, her breasts bare. She was a temptress, every fantasy, every desire he'd ever had come to life.

He curled his hand into a fist, felt the hard bite of his wedding ring. He paused for a moment, lifting his hand to examine it. He pulled it off and set it on the dresser.

Tonight, in this bed, there would be no ghosts from the

past. There would be nothing but Eva and Mak. Nothing but their desire. Their pleasure. He would make sure of that.

He unbuttoned his shirt and discarded it before working at his belt. She was watching him, her eyes rapt on him. He pushed his jeans down his hips, discarding his underwear with them, before joining her on the bed.

He lay across from her, on his side, facing her, and she rolled so that she was facing him, the indent of her waist and flare of her hip even more dramatic and provocative in that pose. She reached out and touched his arm, her fingertips drifting from his bicep to his chest, her light touch skimming over his nipples. His muscles jerked beneath her hand and his erection hardened even more, so hard it was nearly painful now.

He pushed her dress down her hips, taking her panties with it, leaving her completely naked. He couldn't stop looking at her. At her utter perfection. The smoothness of her skin, the roundness of her curves, the dark shadow at the apex of her thighs, her lush breasts.

"You are everything a woman should be," he said.

She reached out and put her hand on his chest. "You're everything, more, than I imagined a man could be, so...maybe we're even?"

"Not even close," he said. "I am outmatched."

She kissed him and for a moment, he was lost in it. He pulled her to him, every bare inch of her against every bare inch of him. She put her leg over his, exposing the heart of her more fully to him, bringing her in even closer.

He moved his hands over her skin, over and over, cupping her butt, relishing every bit of her feminine perfection. She moaned into his mouth and he flipped her to her back, holding himself over her.

Her eyes widened and he dipped his head to kiss the valley between her breasts. "You have to bear with me, *print-*

zyessa," he said, trying to disguise the tremor in his voice, "because I have had a lot of years to think about this moment. And there are things I desire…and I must take my time so I can have all of them."

"I don't…is there time?" she asked. Her voice shook.

"We have all night. Days." He kissed her ribs, her stomach, her hipbone.

"Oh…Mak."

"I like that," he said, smiling against her skin. "My name on your lips. I'll work very hard to make sure I hear it often."

He touched her inner thigh and she parted her legs for him. He pressed a kiss to the tender skin and she shivered. "Mak."

"Like that," he said, kissing her thigh again, closer to her core. "Just like that." He slid his finger over her wetness, as he'd longed to do. He moved his fingers over her clitoris. She responded with a low moan, and he repeated the motion.

Then he dipped his head and tasted her, roaring heat firing through him, igniting his smoldering desire into an inferno. Her hips bucked and he stilled them, using his mouth and fingers on her, his stomach tight with longing.

The need to keep pleasuring her like that forever, the need to take everything with no finesse and no thought for anything but his own desire—they warred with each other, the lusts of his flesh at odds, in ecstasy.

He felt her tense beneath his touch, her body pulsing around his fingers as he continued to lavish attention on her with his tongue. She gripped his shoulders and cried out his name, her voice hoarse, her fingernails biting his skin.

Pride, pleasure so acute it was almost pain, flooded him. He had brought her to the peak, had make her lose herself in her release. He had given Eva all she deserved. And he intended to give her more, even as he took for himself.

He lifted his head, keeping his fingers inside her tight wet body, establishing a rhythm, making sure she stayed ready.

He reached beside him with his other hand and picked up the condom strip, abandoning Eva's pleasure for a moment while he tore off a packet and opened it.

"May I?" She extended her hand, and he gave her the packet. She took the condom out. "First things first," she whispered, wrapping her hand around his naked shaft, squeezing him tightly.

He sucked in a sharp breath, pleasure piercing him.

"Good?" she asked.

"Good doesn't cover it," he said, echoing her earlier words.

She rolled the condom onto his length, her movements slow, methodical, achingly arousing. "Just perfect," she said, a smile on her lips.

He drew her to him and kissed her, lying her back down on the soft bed. She parted her thighs for him, one hand on his back, the other sliding to his butt, urging him on, urging him home. He slid into her slowly, pausing when her breath hitched, letting her grow accustomed to having him inside her. Letting himself acclimate to the feeling of her heat around him.

He gritted his teeth, every muscle in his body so tense it quivered, his arms and thighs shaking as he tried to keep from thrusting into her, hard and fast. When she arched into him, he would give them both more, and when she tensed, he stopped again, giving them both a moment to breathe.

Finally, he was buried inside her, her legs locked around him, a sweet sigh on her lips. He kissed it away, catching the noises of pleasure that escaped, claiming them for himself. Calling his name up from her again and again as he moved inside of her.

The intimacy of it jarred him, the reality of being inside Eva's body far surpassing any fantasy, any depiction on screen or in books. She was surrounding him. Her breath, her voice, her softness, her scent. His world was reduced to her. Was dependent on her.

She stiffened beneath him, her full breasts pushed against his chest, and he felt the pulse of her orgasm around his erection. Deep, raw need overtook him, his thrusts losing all measure of control, all rhythm, as his mind lost its connection with time and space.

There was nothing but Eva. Nothing but her body, their connection.

He let go of everything, everything but the intense feelings rolling through his body. It was like going over the edge of a cliff, release roaring through him as he fell into ultimate, uncontrolled sensation. His chest burned, sensation bursting through him as he found his pleasure.

In the aftermath, he pulled her to him, resting his forehead on hers. She moved her hands over his chest, murmuring words so tender, so sweet, they were like balm, spreading healing over his soul.

He held her as his heart quieted, until his muscles stopped shaking. Until his hands stopped trembling.

In the morning, they might regret it. He would find his way back to his controlled, careful path. There would be recriminations.

But that was for the morning. Tonight he would allow himself to stay lost. Lost in Eva.

It felt better than being found ever had.

CHAPTER TEN

EVA had woken up that morning feeling the same. Turning twenty-one hadn't made her feel any different. But she felt different now.

She turned and looked at Mak. He was on his back, his eyes closed, the lines in his face more shallow as he slept, his expression relaxed. His chest was bare, the hard, cut lines of his muscles exposed, tempting. She traced the ridge that ran down the center of his abs, down to the point covered by the sheet. The bit of fabric rode tantalizingly low, giving her a tease, a taste of the rest of his body without giving it all away.

He was amazing. He'd been amazing. She hadn't realized pleasure like that was possible. Hadn't even had a clue. But he'd blown away every expectation. A smile curved her lips. They'd been explosive. And none of it had come from past experience. None of it from great practiced skill. It had just been…them.

Her stomach fluttered and along with the fluttering came a resurgence of desire. Mak had been beyond fantasy for her. She hoped very much that she'd been the same for him.

She pressed a kiss to his shoulder, her mind replaying everything that had happened since dinner. He stirred beneath the contact, and she kissed him again, letting her fingers join in, drifting over the lines of his stomach.

He shifted beneath her touch, the change in his breathing signaling his return from sleep.

"How come you had to learn to disassemble a bomb?" she asked, the question popping out of her mouth without any thought. But she was curious.

One of his eyes opened and he looked at her. "Just in case. A good skill to have. I only had to use it once."

"On a real bomb?"

"Yes."

"That's horrifying."

"It all worked out. Normally I'm guarding a person, and military tend to handle bombs and other hazards of that nature. But I happened to find one positioned at the entrance of the home of a political official I was guarding. There was no time to wait."

"*Inexperienced* is simply not the right word for you," she said. "You've experienced things I can't even fathom."

He rolled over so quickly she didn't have time to do anything beyond offer a half-hearted squeak of shock, his body covering hers, his hands on either side of her head. "And we're working at remedying things I may not claim proficiency in yet."

"You feel quite proficient to me." She could feel his erection, hardening against the juncture of her thighs.

"You have no one to compare to."

"Don't need to," she said, stretching her neck to kiss his mouth. "Don't want to."

She could happily stay in bed with him forever if she had the chance. If she could freeze one moment and draw it out for as long as she liked, it would be this one. With Mak, so strong and firm on top of her, his gray eyes searing into hers, his heart pounding hard and heavy against her chest.

The kiss caught fire, heat licking through her veins, pooling in her stomach. She was ready for him again. She doubted if there would ever be a time when she wasn't.

She parted her thighs, let him settle down against her. She trapped him, curling her legs around his calves, her hands on his shoulders. She rocked against him, and a muffled curse escaped his lips.

"What?" she whispered.

"If you keep doing that, this will end very quickly."

"That's fine. You lasted admirably the first time."

He took one of her hands from his shoulders and captured it in his, before taking the other one in the same hand and lifting her arms up behind her head so that they were resting on the pillows. And she was powerless. "Admirably, huh?"

"I've heard…not that I've heard much…that some men can't last long enough to give a woman, you know, pleasure. I was prepared for that the first time."

"Really? Well, *printzyessa*, I have had years, and years of practice controlling myself." He dipped his head and took one of her nipples into his mouth. She arched into him, lost in the heat and friction, in the deep pull that started low in her body and radiated through her.

"Then, in the interest of control, maybe you should grab another one of those condoms," she said.

"Good idea."

Happiness had always been a kind of vague, elusive goal. Eva hadn't ever felt truly happy, not since her mother's death or Xander's departure closely after.

And since that horrible arranged marriage to whichever bachelor bid highest had started to get so close to reality, happiness had drifted even farther away.

Maybe Mak was right. Maybe happiness wasn't that important. But right now, sitting in the hot tub, with the warm water shielding her skin from the bitter cold, and Mak's arms around her, her head rested on his hard chest, she felt that happiness had arrived. And she felt as if she didn't want to live another day without it.

"Tell me something," she said, tracing a faint scar that ran along his forearm.

"What?"

She shrugged. "Just something. Anything. Something you've never told anyone before."

He shifted, his arms tightening around her waist, his hand flat on her stomach. "You already have quite a few of my secrets, Eva."

She arched her head back and kissed his throat. "Just a few more."

"You would make a great spy."

"Would I?" she asked, laughing.

"A man would give up anything just to have a kiss from you." His words were light, but there was an undertone of darkness there. One that told her he felt he'd given up something to be with her. And it was more than virginity.

She felt a twinge of guilt, and she tried to block it out. It was needling at her happiness, and she didn't like it. Wouldn't let it.

"Well, I'm not asking you to breach national security."

"All right, but we trade. Prisoner exchange."

"We've already done that," she said. "At least physically. My virginity for yours."

He chuckled. "True enough." He paused for a moment, his fingers playing over her stomach. "I am not an honorable man," he said. The words carried great weight, depth, as though they'd lived in him for years, playing on Repeat. Words that were well-worn in his mind, if not on his tongue.

"I told you to tell me something you hadn't told anyone," she said. "I didn't tell you to lie to me."

"It's true. Would a man of honor give up the care of his

ailing wife to nurses when money allowed it? Would he take job after job, earn more and more money, partly to relieve his responsibility? Because I did. This house...this house was a place for me to come in between some of my jobs. So I could be alone. So I didn't have to see her like that. Alive but not. Caught between the living and the dead and part of neither. I felt as though I was caught there too. And I felt plenty sorry for myself."

"That doesn't mean you weren't honorable. You put everything on hold for her. Honored your marriage vows."

"And I resented them sometimes," he said, an edge in his tone, as though he was desperate to prove he was right.

"So? I resent my life."

"You are right though, about your life. You didn't choose it. I chose mine. And no, it didn't pan out how I planned, but I chose to take Marina away from her family. To marry her when I knew that meant she would lose them."

"Why undermine what you did?" she asked. "Why try to make it seem like it doesn't matter? It did. And who can blame you for needing a break from it?"

"Because I don't deserve a pat on the back for how I acted after a disaster that was of my own making."

"You still blame yourself?"

"Of course."

"You aren't God, Makhail Nabatov, though I'm sure part of you likes to think so."

"So is that who I blame then? God? Would that solve my problems? If I could wash my hands of it all and claim divine intervention?"

She shook her head. "No. If you have to blame someone, blame the driver of the other car. Blame doesn't help. It doesn't get anyone anywhere. It...I have another brother, you know."

He stiffened. "Yes, I saw something about him, briefly, when going over your information."

"You won't find very much about Alexander. Because he won't come back to Kyonos. My father, in his search for blame after the death of my mother, chose Xander as the scapegoat. I think even Stavros believes it. It's very likely Xander does too."

"How?" Mak asked.

"Because Xander was driving the car when it crashed, with my mother in it. They were out driving along the beach because Xander wanted to learn to drive and my mother lived to accommodate him. Xander was always the fun one, the impetuous one. He was very like my mother, you know. But it was such a normal thing. She took her son out for a drive. That's all. Like you, they encountered a driver who wasn't paying attention. Would you blame Xander?"

"No. But it's different."

"It's not."

He shifted and turned her, making the water spray around them. "You are stubborn," he ground out.

She leaned in and kissed the tip of his nose. "I know. And so are you. But you have to let it go, Mak. How long will you carry the pain with you?"

His dark eyebrows locked together. "I don't know how to let go. If I let go, it's like she never existed."

Eva shook her head. "Don't forget her. But remember her smile. Remember what you loved about her."

He winced. "Love is not my favorite memory." He trailed his fingers over the damp line of Eva's collarbone. "But I can remember her smile."

"Good. Hold onto that."

He studied her for a moment. "You're the only woman I've ever met who would ask her lover to think of the face of another woman."

"She was your wife. I respect that. You…whether you want to remember it or not, you loved her."

"I have called you many things, not all of them flattering. But now, I just want to say that you are the most amazing woman I have ever met," he said.

Tears filled her eyes and she hoped he wouldn't notice. Hoped the water droplets on her skin would help conceal them. "You're the most amazing man I've ever met. So maybe we're even."

"Not even. Not even close." He brushed his thumb over her cheek, over the tears that had started to fall. Blessedly, he didn't comment. "Ready to go in?"

"Yes," she said. "Ready."

"An indoor picnic?" Mak asked a few hours later when he walked into the living area. He was freshly showered and shaved and he smelled like clean skin and sex.

News to Eva that sex had a smell. But she knew it now. And she was finding that she liked it.

"Well, it would be impractical to have an outdoor picnic," she said, running her palm over the blanket that was spread over the living-room carpet, just in front of the fire. "Unless you fancy the idea of sitting on a blanket in the snow."

"Not really. What inspired this?"

"Well, if we're still sharing secrets…this is something I've always wanted to do. Part of my epic romantic fantasy, if you will."

"Is it?"

"Yes. Come and sit down."

He gave her a half smile and walked over to the blanket, sitting down next to her. "All right. Now explain this epic romantic fantasy."

"In my mind, when I thought of romance, I pictured picnics and dancing. Well, we've danced. And now we'll picnic.

In lieu of a green field dotted with daisies, I've opted for an oatmeal carpet and warmth."

"Good choice." He paused for a moment, his eyes intense on hers. "But don't weave too many romantic fantasies around me."

Her throat tightened. *Too late.* "Of course not. We both know what this is."

Except she wasn't sure she knew what it was, not really. She felt too much for it to be a fling. Or was that normal? She couldn't be sure. Her seasonal friends had flings, and they spoke of it with a sort of light humor. But Eva didn't feel any humor in regards to Mak. She couldn't imagine recounting intimate details of their time together over coffee, while laughing.

It felt too private. Too personal. It was hers. Theirs.

"Good," he said, picking up a plate and starting on his chicken.

She suddenly didn't feel very hungry. Still, she made a show of chewing on a piece of bread for longer than was strictly necessary.

This was a fantasy, and she knew it. At least, she vaguely knew it. Knew that when their time in the chalet ended, they ended too. Knew that this was borrowed time at its most precious and brief. But she wished she didn't know it.

When she went back, there would, potentially, be another man waiting for her. The man she was supposed to share forever with.

It was cruel. She had this little window of time with Mak, and then after that, eternity with a husband she didn't care about.

Now her appetite really was gone.

"Are you all right?" he asked.

"Uh, yes. Really. Fine." Breaking apart inside, but she'd survive. She had no other choice.

"Good. This dinner is good."

"Liesel made it. I can't claim any credit."

"Ah. Did she go home for the evening?"

"Yes," Eva said. "'I think I want dessert."

"You've barely touched dinner."

"That's fine. I don't want it." She reached beneath the edge of the blanket and pulled out a condom packet. "Dessert first will suit me just fine," she said, holding it out to him.

He set his plate on the couch, his eyes blank, guarded. "You had a plan for the evening. Another part of your long-held fantasy?"

She shook her head. "No. This is new. I had some pretty girlish fantasies. But now…well, now I know what it means to really want someone. To want you. And that's a lot more important than food to me right now."

It went beyond a physical hunger though. She needed the connection, needed him to be joined to her, to be inside her. Needed to be connected to him. She needed something to make her feel whole, to stop the endless, empty ache that was spreading through her.

He stood and she did too. He tugged the edge of the blanket, clearing the space in front of the fireplace before walking to her, taking her in his arms and kissing her as if she was the best thing he'd tasted all day.

She wrapped her arms around his neck and kissed him back, pouring everything into it. Her fear, her frustration, her passion.

He unzipped her dress and it fell to her feet. She pushed it aside and kept kissing him while she tugged his shirt up over his head, running her hands over his sculpted chest, his chest hair prickling her palms as she explored his body. She would never get enough of him. He was beautiful, sculpted and lean, the ultimate fantasy.

But it wasn't about that. That might have sparked her initial attraction, but his beauty came from somewhere else, somewhere deeper. Whether he saw it in himself or not, it didn't matter. She did.

They took turns discarding clothes, between kisses and sighs, and when he laid her down on the blanket, she looked at him for a long time, her hands stroking his cheeks, his lips, tracing the line of his jaw.

Words hovered on her lips. Words she was too scared to speak, too scared even to think. She didn't want to know what they were, not exactly, or why they felt as though they would burst from her if she didn't bite down hard on her lower lip.

"What's wrong?" he asked.

She shook her head, too afraid to speak. Too afraid of what she might say.

"Ready?" he asked.

She nodded, pressing a kiss to his forehead. He slid inside her and she let her head fall back, pleasure coursing through her as he filled her, as the empty ache that had been plaguing her abated. Each thrust of his body into hers pushed her higher, made her feel as if she was standing on the edge of a cliff, afraid to jump. Afraid not to.

When she gave in, let go, she felt herself falling, pleasure rushing up to greet her. Too much. Too fast. She gripped his shoulders, trying to find an anchor, something to keep her from losing herself entirely.

Not even that worked. The world fragmented, broke apart. She broke too, along with everything around her, slipping away from time and place as pleasure filled in the cracks, taking the place of reality, becoming more important, more real than anything around her. More important than the future, than the past. There was only now. Only this.

She wished it could last forever.

She clung to it, even as things slowly started to right themselves. As the fragments were put back together, as it all came back, clear and sharp.

The carpet was against her back, the fire hot on one side of her. Mak was above her, his breathing harsh as he shuddered out his own release, every muscle in his body tense, her name on his lips.

I love you.

The words burst into her mind, loud, undeniable. She closed her eyes and tried to ignore them, tried to shut them out as they echoed through her body.

She wasn't supposed to love him. She was only supposed to want him. To take his body, to satisfy a physical desire. She wasn't supposed to feel that she would die if he wasn't with her. Wasn't supposed to feel whole for the first time.

It couldn't work. It wouldn't. Even if everything was set aside that her father had planned for her, Mak had made it very clear that he didn't want love. Didn't need it.

But all those things that had left him littered with scars, they were the reasons she loved him. Now that she'd acknowledged it, she couldn't seem to stop.

He pulled her into his arms, and he didn't speak. She said a silent prayer of thanks and curled up against him, listening to his heart pounding against her cheek.

This was all she would ever have of him. And it would have to be enough.

Somehow, it would have to be.

CHAPTER ELEVEN

"Your father called." Mak was standing at the edge of the living room, backlit by the light in the entryway, the hard lines of his body visible. He was naked. Gorgeous. A fine first sight.

Eva came to full consciousness slowly, groggy and, she was certain, with carpet print embedded into her cheek. She and Mak had fallen asleep in front of the fireplace, both of them too lethargic to make their way upstairs.

"What did he say?" she asked, sitting, tugging the picnic blanket, which they'd commandeered as makeshift comforter for the night, up to her breasts.

"He's ready for us to come back. The media haven't dropped the story, and what he thinks they need is your presence." Mak's voice was blank of emotion, his facial expression just as impossible to read.

"But I thought...I didn't think having me there while the media was storming the castle was what anyone wanted I...I certainly don't want to get hounded by reporters." She didn't want her time with Mak to end. That was the main problem. Reporters didn't really scare her, but going back to her cloistered life at the palace, that did frighten her.

"I...will you stay?" she asked.

Silence hung between them.

When Mak spoke, he spoke slowly. "I'm not through protecting you. Now that the media might hassle you, I suppose there's even more of a reason for me to be there."

"And I might run away. Or cause more scandal," she said, looking for reasons to reinforce his being there.

He laughed, a hollow sound. "Somehow I don't believe that. But I will stay."

"Good," she said.

She could face everything, even the press, if Mak was there. And even if they could never sleep in each other's arms again, she would rather have him close by than not have him at all.

She looked at the empty space next to her and felt her heart squeeze tight. She wished she had known that last night was the last night. She might have held him closer.

She might not have slept.

She looked at Mak, standing across the room from her, his posture formal, nothing in his face hinting at his emotions, or even if he had them.

If she had known that last night had been the last time, she might even have told him how she felt.

So it was probably good she hadn't known.

"I'll go and gather my things," she said, standing up, tugging the blanket around her body.

She started to walk past him, then stopped, turning to face him. She studied the lines of his face, so familiar, so essential. She pulled the blanket more securely around her body and stood up on her toes, pressing a kiss to his lips. He froze for a moment, the put one hand on her waist, holding her to him as he returned the kiss. As he slid his tongue against hers, taking the kiss deep, intense. Desperate.

Her heart pounded hard, echoing in her head, her entire body shaking as she squeezed her eyes closed. She needed this kiss, this last kiss, to last her forever.

It wasn't enough. It would never be enough.

When they parted they were both breathing hard, Mak's eyes glittering with emotion now, deep and dark and unnameable.

She felt a tear slide down her cheek and she didn't bother to wipe it away. She wouldn't hide how he affected her. But she wouldn't crumble either.

"Now I'll go and get ready," she said, trying to force a smile.

"I'll meet you down here in half an hour," he said, his voice a whisper.

"See you then."

Mak spent the flight in the seat at the opposite end of the plane from Eva's seat. He had to gather his control. Had to find a way to put some distance between them.

They were about to stand before King Stephanos, about to rejoin the real world.

He didn't often question his actions. Since the car accident that had cost Marina her life, at least a real life, he had simply moved on. Tried to make what he had, what they had, work.

He should question the actions he'd taken with Eva. He should denounce them. Regret them. Something.

He didn't. He couldn't.

She was the first woman to truly test his control. There had been others who were willing, especially since he'd been able to act on any desires he might have. But nothing about the moment, or the person, had felt right. He'd felt dead. Bored.

With Eva he felt alive. As if she'd breathed into him, made him see things in color. She added an indefinable something to his life, to each moment. And he felt starved for it, for her, always.

Still, he should feel regret. He could offer her nothing, not just because of her likely-impending marriage, but because he had nothing to give. Nothing at all. He was dry. Spent.

He could give endlessly to his job, a job that only made physical demand of him, and he could keep Eva happy in bed endlessly too. But she needed more. She was so beautiful, so untouched, even by the tragedy that had happened in her own life.

She didn't need someone so damaged. Especially when he knew he could do nothing but take. And he'd been there. He'd been the one to give, and had given until it was all gone. His life blood leached from him, leaving nothing but a shell in place of the man he'd been.

He wouldn't do that to her. Ever. An arranged marriage with a man who had the possibility of giving her everything she needed was a much better thing for her.

Even if the idea of another man's hands on her body gave him the impression of hot, dry ash on his tongue.

"What are we going to tell him?" Eva's voice came from just behind him.

He turned. "Nothing. Your father, I assume? But even if you mean the pope, the answer is still nothing."

"Not a believer in confession?"

"Not confessing something of this nature."

"Are you ashamed?"

He stood and braced himself on the back of the chair, a fierce anger erupting in him. At her. At himself. "I am attached to every body part I have. And I don't fancy losing any. Neither do I fancy spending any time in a Kyonosian jail cell for violating their precious princess."

"They all think I've been violated before anyway. Besides, we both know you could escape from a jail cell in what? Five minutes?"

He shrugged. "Ten maybe."

"Exactly."

He wanted to touch her, but he wouldn't. That path led to

madness. To ruin. "That doesn't mean I'm eager to go in and make any announcements."

"I know," she said, her voice much more subdued than he was accustomed to hearing it.

"Tell me your favorite thing about Kyonos," he said. He wanted to keep her from thinking too much. From feeling sad. Especially when they both knew exactly what likely awaited her back home.

She blinked rapidly. "I like…I like the sea. The heat. The cafés. I like that it isn't covered in snow." Her voice thickened. "I like that I can go outside whenever I want without worrying about frostbite. And that I don't have to sit by a fireplace to get warm."

"And you have your own room?" he asked, pain lancing his chest.

"Yes. For as long as I have my own room, I'll treasure it. Until the day I'm forced into marriage. Into sharing it with someone I don't know or care about. Until that day, there will be things I enjoy about Kyonos. About life. I'll get back to you after that."

She turned and walked back to her seat, her posture stiff. And Mak tried not to wonder when he'd started feeling things again.

She'd lied. Big-time. There was nothing comforting about home. Truthfully, there was nothing home about home. It was nothing but a castle built for ancestors long dead, to impress the outside world, and to imprison those who lived in it.

At least some of the people who lived in it.

She tried not to flinch as she walked through the vast open doors that led into the foyer of the castle. High ceilings, built that high for the express purpose of making those who'd just walked across the hallowed threshold feel very, very small.

She was determined not to let it work. That didn't mean

it wasn't working a little bit, but she was trying to make it so that it didn't.

Mak was behind her, his presence solid. Comforting. Intoxicating. Everything it shouldn't be. She couldn't lean on Mak. She had to draw strength from herself. Even so, she ached for a partner. Not a support, but someone who would stand beside her, an active participant in what she was about to do. Not a passive soldier who simply walked ten paces behind, his emotions cut off. His body present, his heart cold as stone.

It was just before noon and there was staff everywhere, hurrying around them paying her very little attention. The staff weren't wild about her, not because of any personal dealings but because she caused trouble in the well-ordered world of the palace. Anyone who made King Stephanos unhappy indirectly made them unhappy, after all.

She continued, head down, toward her father's office, trying to ignore the prickle of heat on the back of her neck, the racing of her heart that told her Mak was keeping pace with her.

She stopped at the door to the king's office. She only thought of him as The King when she knew he was going to issue an edict she didn't like. And something inside her told her that he was about to.

"Shall I go with you?" It was the first time Mak had spoken since the plane landed.

"No," she said. "I'll handle it. After all, it isn't as though we've been caught out." She turned the door handle and stepped into the room. "Father, I'm home."

Stephanos didn't look up from the papers in front of him. "Good. We have to act quickly."

"We do?"

"Yes." He looked up then, pulling his glasses off. "The press is tearing you apart. You're quickly becoming a running joke. Some are quite clever though none bear repeating in polite company."

Eva swallowed and straightened her shoulders. "As long as it's done cleverly. I'd hate to think the jokes were stupid as well as vulgar."

"Be that as it may, there may be a chance to save you yet."

She looked left, then right. "Is there a priest around?"

Her father treated her to an expression that was decidedly lacking in amusement. "There will be soon enough. Bastian Van Saant has agreed to go forward with the marriage and I have accepted his offer for your hand."

Eva's ears crackled, then fuzzed out, as though she was getting bad reception on a radio station. Her father's lips were still moving, but she could only make out a few words, sprinkled throughout waves of oppressive silence.

"Four weeks."

That she heard, loud and clear. Her six-month window had been drastically reduced.

The room pitched violently to the side. Except nothing was out of order, everything on her father's desk was still laid out precisely, and her feet were still solidly planted on the whitewashed stone floor. Everything was as it should be. Everything around her. Everything in her screamed like a wounded animal.

Marrying Bastian had always seemed wrong. The idea of marrying him now...after falling for Mak, after giving all of herself, body, heart and soul to him—it was repulsive.

"I need to go," she said, her own voice as fuzzy and distant as her father's.

She stumbled out of the office and past Mak, down the long, winding corridor and out the glass parlor doors into the garden. Air, maybe the air would help. She breathed in deeply, waiting for the salt and brine to penetrate the horrible fog that had descended.

It did. And when it did it left the cold sting of reality in its place. Harsh, painful, bright, like the white sunlight that pounded down on the grass. She kept walking, stumbled down the path and into the alcove shielded by grapevines.

She dropped to her knees and simply stayed. She waited, for tears, for something. There was nothing. She closed her eyes and opened her mouth, willing a sound of pain to come out, to relieve some of the pressure inside of her.

But it wouldn't come. She was frozen, trapped in herself. All she could manage to do was gulp in air in halting gasps, a feeling of panic gripping her, holding her down.

A hand on her shoulder, warm and comforting, drew her back from the abyss. "What happened?"

She tried to swallow more air, but couldn't find any way to speak.

Mak knelt down with her, his hand sliding over her back, around her shoulders, drawing her to him. She rested her head on his chest and breathed in deeply. She memorized his smell, the way his heart sounded beneath her ear, the way he breathed. Why had she thought she could just say goodbye? That it could end? How had she not realized just what the separation would mean? How badly it would hurt?

Mak pulled her up onto his lap, settling in his black suit in the dust, uncaring for the expensive fabric.

She clung to him. She hadn't wanted support earlier. Hadn't wanted to do anything beyond standing on her own feet. But right now, she needed to be held up. Just for now. And she was glad she had him.

She didn't know what she would do when Mak wasn't there to keep her from falling.

CHAPTER TWELVE

ONLY madness could come from this. From touching her. He had sworn he would let it go. Let her go. That those last moments in the chalet would be his last moments of insanity.

Because she needed him. Because she had no one else. Because he *needed* to.

Touching her like this, without touching her the way he truly desired, was a new kind of torture. It should be old and familiar now, the denial of his body's needs. But this wasn't the same. This was about closeness. About her skin against his.

He wouldn't. He would just hold her.

He moved his hands over her back, frustrated at the feel of silk beneath his fingers, instead of soft, bare skin.

He held her like that for a long time. Then she stiffened, pulling away from him and moving into a standing position.

"There's no use crying about it," she said, wiping her cheeks. "It's done."

"It's not done yet," he said.

"It's as good as done." She looked at him, the depth of emotion in her eyes stabbing him straight in the heart. "What other option do I have?"

His chest seized tight. "Eva…I can't…"

"I'm not asking you to rescue me, Mak. I'm not locked in a tower. Look…doors everywhere, I could walk out if I liked. But I don't know why I would. For…fun? You've said it many times, happiness is transient but doing something for the right reasons, something rooted in honor, that means something, doesn't it?"

"It's supposed to," he said. Unsure now if it was true. Unsure that it meant anything.

"So I'm trying to matter. Trying to help erase the scandal I put on my family name. Trying to do something right for my country." She blinked rapidly. "And I hope….I hope it's enough."

She turned and walked out of the courtyard. He felt as if the color went with her.

He wanted to tell her he was wrong, to tell her to be happy. But he didn't know the first thing about finding happiness. How could he direct her to find something he wasn't certain existed?

She'd made her choice. She would marry Bastian.

And he would find a way to rebuild the walls that had surrounded his heart for so many years.

Go out. Have fun. Or at least pretend you're having fun.

That was Eva's directive. She and Mak were on assignment. Going to shop in the city without any scandal cropping up. Mak was supposed to shadow her, keep the press from mobbing her and, Eva was certain, keep her in line.

It was silly, but she was desperate for the car ride. Desperate for the moment when the door would close and she and Mak would be alone. She liked their arrangement, where it was just the two of them.

When Mak settled in beside her and they were closed into their bubble, a knot tightened in her stomach. "I…I didn't think, Mak. Should I ask a driver to take us in one of the larger cars? You don't like driving and I…"

"I'm fine, Eva," he said.

"I wanted to be alone with you. Just for a bit," she said, quietly, as he started the engine.

"Is there really any point to that?"

"No. I suppose not. Although, maybe there is. It's nice to be with someone you…" She stumbled over her words. "…like a lot."

"Is that so?" His tone was filled with bland disinterest. Just as it had been in the beginning.

"It is."

He put the car into gear and started driving away from the palace. They were silent for a while, then Mak spoke. "So what is it you like about me?" he asked. A strange question coming from Mak. One that revealed a vulnerability she wasn't accustomed to seeing.

"A lot of things," she said. "You don't complain if you have to prepare your own food, which is rare."

"Really?" he asked dryly.

"In royal circles it's very rare," she said. "And I like talking to you. You're judgmental sometimes, but you listen anyway. Also rare."

"You flatter me."

"I'm not trying to."

"I guessed."

A bubble of happiness started to fill up in Eva's chest. She was with Mak and they were talking. And the wedding was four whole weeks away. In her mind, she imagined that date stretching far into the future. Visualized twenty-eight days lasting as long as possible.

Mak pulled the car up to a boutique that offered valet parking and put the car in Park with the keys still in the ignition. "Anything else?"

Eva unbuckled and paused, then pulled on the door handle. "You're very good in bed." She opened the door and got out, closing it behind her, heart pounding a bit faster than normal.

She heard the driver's side door slam, and then heard Mak barking orders to the valet before stalking after her. She didn't turn to look at him as she strode into the boutique, all of her efforts focused on ignoring him. Keeping her eyes in front of her.

She paused at a rack of sweaters.

"Careful, Eva," Mak growled out the words as he walked by her, headed into the back of the shop to do that blending he was so good at.

"No thanks," she said sweetly.

A shop assistant came over to Eva, her eyes widening, mouth falling open for a brief moment before she made a quick recovery, as she realized who Eva was. Once the discovery was made, clothes were brought out en masse. She wasn't trying to fly under the radar, which was an odd experience, and she wasn't making use of the family stylist, which was equally rare.

Mak stayed on the fringes, keeping his eyes on her, but staying away from her and the saleswoman as they systematically made their way through the jeans, tops, slacks and skirts.

"And I need a gown," Eva said, aware she was about to invite speculation. "A very special event. One we're planning at the last minute."

The official announcement that was happening over the weekend. The one where she would have to pretend she felt something for Bastian. The one that would cement everything in place.

"How exciting!" The girl did a little clap and ran to the rack of gowns.

Eva watched Mak's face as she tried the gowns on, one by one: some with structured bodices, some with filmy skirts that clung to her legs. One was nearly backless.

Mak's jaw was tight, his hands clenched at his sides, his eyes blank. And she knew it was because he wanted her. Because the heat that was crackling between them was palpable, even from across the room.

It was a strange mix of heaven and hell, knowing Mak wanted her as he did. Knowing it when she couldn't have him. When he couldn't make good on the promise in his eyes. It made her body ache, made her hands tremble.

She turned slightly in the cream-colored gown she was wearing, so that Mak could see her from the side, feigning interest in the mirror. "You don't think it's too low?" she asked.

It was strapless with good structure beneath a layer of filmy chiffon. The neck scooped down, revealing quite a bit of cleavage, the color making her golden skin glow.

"No, it's lovely. Just the right amount of sexy," the saleswoman offered.

"Great. Then this is it." She could see Mak swallow hard. "I'll take all of this," she said, indicating the clothing that filled an entire rack that stretched across the dressing area. "Mak," she said, directing her attention to him. "Can you arrange the details?"

One dark eyebrow arched and he stood, walking over to where she was. "I should think you're quite capable."

"Mmm. Quite, but I don't carry this much money. I thought you might have some means of using my father's credit card?"

"No." He turned to the saleswoman. "I've got it." He took a wallet from his inside jacket pocket and pulled out a credit card. One with his name on it. "Charge it all. She'll take…" His eyes landed on a short, silvery dress that was on a mannequin. "…that one too."

The other woman's eyes widened. "Of course, Mr.…."

"Nabatov."

"Right." She took the plastic and headed to the back of the store, where she could handle something as bourgeois as money in private.

"What was that about?" she asked, when they were alone.

"Is the dress for him?"

"No," she said tartly. "It's for you."

"Why?"

"I don't know," she said. "Anyway, why did you...pay?"

He shrugged. "Because I can."

"Still, you're going to start rumors."

"Possible."

Eva's eyes were glittering with fire, and Mak couldn't deny he was intrigued. He'd been stupid, producing his card and paying for her clothes. A surge of possessiveness, intense and dark, had taken over. A kind of possessiveness he'd never known he had the capacity to feel.

To show that she belonged to him in some way—a foolish thought. He crushed the things in his life. Broke the things he loved.

The word, the one he tried never to say, never to think, assaulted him. Tore at him like a rabid dog. He denied it. Tried to harden himself against the attack.

"You don't care, do you?"

"Not a bit," he said.

"So much for protecting my reputation."

"That ship has sailed, don't you think? Sunk, actually," he said.

"I'm rebuilding it. In fact it's set to float in about four weeks."

The saleswoman came back with dollar signs in her eyes, clearly happy with the total, and her expected commission. "We can have all of it delivered to the palace for you," she said.

"Do that," Mak said. "And add a tip." He named a figure that made the woman's jaw drop.

"Thank you," she said.

"I'll come back sometime," Eva said.

Mak could sense her loss of elation, the settling in of reality. Eva, for all that she was playing her smiley happy self, was not happy. And he could feel it.

"Ready?" he asked.

"More than." The light in her eyes had dimmed. She'd even lost that little spark of mischief, the one that had flared when she was teasing him. When she'd been sure she was playing casual, trying to make her flashes of cleavage look accidental.

"So am I," he said, the words hard to force out around the tightening in his throat. When her thoughts turned to her impending marriage, and he was certain they had, it made a kind of feral rage boil inside of him.

The thought of another man's hands on her body...it couldn't happen. She had branded him, marked his body with her touch. For him, there could be no other woman. The thought hit him with a certainty he'd only felt once before.

Just as he'd known he would honor his vows, care for Marina until she'd taken her last breath, he knew he was committed to Eva. The very idea of another lover seemed wrong.

Sex, for him, could never be about a simple physical release. It had become something sacred in his mind. His experiences with Eva had confirmed it.

But she would take Bastian. He would be her husband. In every way.

Mak gritted his teeth. "Let's go. Outside."

He opened the door for her and followed her out, checking all sides of her, watching for any possible threat. The car was delivered within minutes and he opened the door for her before getting in on the driver's side.

"I hope now you're happy. You have some clothes that you chose. Clothes that are you." He gunned the engine and merged with traffic, taking a sharp right, headed back in the direction of the palace.

"You...you remembered me saying that," she said, her voice filled with shock.

"I remember everything you've said." He meant it to come out harsh, a reminder that he didn't forget things. That details, in his mind, were imperative. It came out soft. More a reminder that she was special than anything else.

"Me too," she said.

A good thing, since very soon, memories would be all either of them had.

CHAPTER THIRTEEN

THE engagement party was a glittering affair. No formal announcement had been made, but rumors had been rampant from the moment it had leaked that there was going to be an event held at the palace on short notice.

The guest list had been kept brief, accommodating only the most influential families from Kyonos and from Bastian's country, Komenia.

Eva hung back, peering into the ballroom from the outside, watching the party at a distance. No one noticed or cared. They wanted gossip, they wanted to be seen. And once they realized the event centered around her, then they might care about her presence. But until then, she was another face in attendance.

It was well known that she was a rebel. The youngest. The least influential. She wondered if that would change when she had a husband with power.

The thought galled. That she would matter more because of the man she married.

A man she wasn't even tempted to scan the room for. No, the man she was looking for was one of the people she hadn't seen since she'd arrived.

The back of her neck prickled. She turned, the chiffon of her ball gown swirling around her legs as she did. Mak was there, looking harder, leaner. Looking like a stranger. Except for his eyes. Eyes she'd always taken to be emotionless. But she knew now, suddenly and with clarity, that that wasn't true.

It was simply emotion too deep to read easily.

"You look beautiful," he said.

"Thank you. So do you." She indicated his custom-cut suit, her heart thundering as she took him in. He was so perfect. And tonight, any dream she harbored of a future with him ended.

"Do you know how things are going tonight?" he asked.

"Yes. In an hour my father will make the announcement and Bastian and I will go and allow him to present us before the guests. The engagement will be...official then."

"I see. So you have some time?"

"Yes."

"Come with me."

She didn't know what he wanted or why he wanted it. She didn't really care. She just wanted to be with him. It didn't matter if it was for five minutes, or for an eternity. No, it did matter. She wanted forever, it was just that she wouldn't be getting it.

"Where?"

"The garden."

He held out his hand and she took it, warmth rushing through her as his fingers closed around hers. That simple touch spread a bone-deep ache through her body, a need that transcended anything she'd ever known. And it wasn't just sex. It was something more, something deeper. Something that frightened her because she knew that soon, very soon, she would be denied Mak's touch in even the simplest capacity.

He led her through the vacant corridor. They passed staff, members of security. But staff was paid to ignore what they weren't meant to see, and Mak was the superior of every security team member there. That meant no one questioned them. They hardly looked.

They went out into the garden behind the glittering ball-room. People were milling around on the balcony, chatting, laughing and drinking, the sounds filling the night air. She and Mak skirted the outside of the trees, walking deep into the garden, to their place, hidden back in the grapevines.

It was the last place he'd held her in his arms. The place she'd given in to despair. The place where her hope had left her. He'd come to her then, braced her, helped her stay strong.

"Dance with me," she said, her voice trembling.

"I should not," he said.

"We shouldn't be here at all. We're courting impropriety, and we're doing it very deliberately."

"That's true."

"Dance with me like you did the night at the ball. In the beginning." Rather than here, at the end. Her stomach ached and she closed her eyes against the pain.

He drew her to him, pressing her body against the length of his. "Very true," he whispered.

She laid her head on his chest and listened to his heart pound beneath her ear. She wanted to tell him, so badly. The words hovered on the edge of her lips, sweet on her tongue, but threatening to burn her if she released them.

If he rejected her love, it would ruin what they had. They could never be together. Not really. So it was better to just preserve it as it was. To hold the love she felt for him close to her chest. To use it to warm her through her cold marriage. And maybe someday it wouldn't be Mak's face she saw when she closed her eyes.

Doubtful. But maybe.

It made her want to cling to his image even more tightly.

They swayed, not keeping time. There was no music here, no noise from her engagement party reaching in to disturb them. She pushed back the despair that was threatening to crowd in. There was no room for it now. This was her time, her moment.

"Back at the chalet, I thought that moment in the living room would be our last kiss," he said, his voice rough.

She swallowed. "So did I."

"I don't want it to be our last kiss."

"I don't either." She didn't want there to be a last kiss, she wanted there always to be another kiss on the horizon. To have years of them. To fall asleep to them and wake up to them. But no one ever asked what she wanted.

He tilted his head and brushed her lips with his. Every pore of her body sighed with relief. For now, there would be more kisses. Maybe too many to count. And she would take that. Happily.

He deepened the kiss and she met him, sliding her tongue against his, spreading her hands over his shoulders, down his back, holding him to her, as he tightened his hold on her.

A sob climbed her throat, but she suppressed it. She didn't have time to cry. She couldn't waste one moment of this time with him by being sad, or by regretting what wasn't to be. She had to seize now. She had to live in it completely.

She loosened his tie and undid the top four buttons on his shirt, spreading it as wide as she could so she could reach her hand in and brush her fingers over his muscles, letting them follow the contours of his body, the gorgeous, defined lines that were so sexy they made her hands tremble.

He slid his hands down her waist, to her hips, gathering the gauzy fabric of her gown in his hands and bunching it into his hands, moving the hemline from the ground to her mid calf. She tilted her head and he kissed her neck, her shoulder, running his tongue along the edge of her gown's neckline.

She shivered beneath the sensual friction and he brought the hem of her gown up higher, to her knees, before lowering one hand and sweeping it beneath the fabric. He moved his hand up her thigh, cupping her bare hip, finding her panties and drawing them down. She kicked them to the side and he moved his hand around to palm her butt.

"Please tell me you came prepared for this," she said as he walked her backward toward the stone bench.

"I did. Though I'm not certain that's something I should be proud of."

"I'm happy about it," she said, trying to lighten the moment, trying to move some of the heavy weight off of her chest.

"That's a relief."

She sat on the bench and he knelt before her, pushing her dress up past her hips, exposing her body to his gaze. He leaned in and pressed a kiss to her inner thigh. She shivered, anticipation tightening her stomach. He'd done this quite a few times during their stay in Switzerland, and he never disappointed.

He zeroed in on her most sensitive spot, his tongue lavishing her with attention on that one place that sent waves rippling through her entire body. She could feel herself getting close to the edge, feel her orgasm building, like water contained by a splintering wall of glass. Slowly, slowly, building pressure.

He reached into his back pocket and took out his wallet, fishing a condom out of one of the sections.

"You're a regular pro," she said, trying not to sound, or feel, too bad.

"Necessity," he said.

She reached for his belt buckle and undid it, her fingers shaking as she pushed it through the loops and opened his fly. She could see the outline of his erection pressing against his underwear. She pressed her palm over his hardened flesh, testing his weight.

His breath hissed through his teeth and he moved nearer to

her. She pushed his underwear over his shaft, encircling him with her fingers, squeezing him. He handed her the packet, and she tore it open, rolling the condom down over his length.

The pause in full-on contact had helped some of the pressure ease, but the moment his body was back up against hers, his hardness pressing against her, it all crashed over her again.

She hooked her legs over his hips and he angled himself, pushing inside her slowly.

"Oh, Mak," she said, wrapping her arms around his neck, hiding her face against his shoulder as a deep, overwhelming sense of satisfaction spread through her.

"Eva," he ground out, his hand on her lower back, drawing her forward. She tilted her head back and looked at him, completely captured by the expression of dark sensuality etched into every line of his face.

He thrust into her, his eyes never leaving hers, unless he was leaning in to kiss her lips, to whisper hot, forbidden words in her ear.

Every thrust, every word, pushed her higher, put more cracks in her control, until it all burst, pleasure rushing through her. Uncontrollable, unstoppable. Mak's pace increased, every movement forcing a small aftershock every time his body pressed against hers.

He froze against her, a harsh sound escaping his lips as he dropped his hand from her back, his palm braced hard on the bench as he embraced his own release.

She cupped his face in her hand, moving her fingers over his sweat-dampened skin, pushing her fingers through his thick hair. A tear slid down her cheek and she didn't even try to stop it.

"How much time," she whispered, her throat so tight it was almost impossible to speak.

He shifted, his focus drifting to his watch. "Twenty minutes."

Her chest trembled, shaking as she held a sob at bay. "Okay." She pushed gently on his shoulders.

He stood, turning and rounding a corner for a moment, returning a moment later with his clothes righted, the condom discarded.

She stood then, her knees unsteady, and brushed the front and back of her dress, trying to make sure everything was lying as it should. Checking to see if her hair was in place, her bodice tugged up where it should be.

He tucked a strand of hair behind her ear, letting his hand hover by her cheek for a moment before curling his fingers into a fist and dropping it at his side.

"I'll escort you back."

She nodded. "Okay."

The walk back seemed so much shorter than the walk into the garden had been. They came out of the foliage and back into the light, the noise of the party.

She went through the same door they'd used to exit the palace. The corridor was strangely empty now. She looked at the door to the ballroom, partially opened. She could see impressions of people moving around inside. Waiting for the announcement. Waiting for her.

"Eva," Mak said, his voice broken. "I'm sorry. That was…"

She pulled back from him, feeling a break between them, anger tightening her chest. "Don't. Don't apologize to me for what just happened. Don't apologize for any of it. Ever."

She walked away from him, toward the ballroom…closer. She stopped just outside the door. Her feet felt stuck to the spot. She turned and looked at Mak, a shiver racking her body, even though she felt no cold.

Bastian walked out of a side door, his fair good looks stirring nothing in her but the desire to run. To run toward Mak. She looked from her soon-to-be-fiancé, back to the man she loved, Mak, who was standing with hands at his sides, his expression one of barely suppressed violence.

"Evangelina, are you ready?" Bastian asked, his tone so polite, so detached, that not even the use of her name seemed personal.

She looked back at Mak, willing him to stop things. Willing him to ask her to stay. He didn't. He only stood, frozen, watching her, his eyes cold. "Yes."

She took his arm and headed into the ballroom with him, leaving her heart outside in the corridor, with a man she loved more than words could express.

She felt sick. She felt wrong. Her entire body felt branded by Mak, and now she had her arm looped through another man's. Her body still ached, her lips were still swollen from kissing Mak. She felt as if what she had done, what she desired, was scrawled across her face for anyone to see.

She wanted to run. Away from Bastian. Away from everything.

But Mak was about honor. Mak lived it, he breathed it. Every line in his face spoke of the desire to go after her. But she knew he wouldn't.

He had just broken every rule. For her. She knew he wouldn't do it again. And she could never ask him to.

Because this was about more than one person. It was about the alliance of countries. It was about duty. And she knew that in Mak's world, duty reigned. It was one of the things that made him so wonderful. One of the things that made him the man she loved.

She turned her back on love and turned toward duty. The pain coursing through her body protesting each step she took into the ballroom. Each step she took away from the life she desired, and into a life she would never have chosen. A life she would never be able to escape.

* * *

"The wedding will take place in just over three weeks." King Stephanos made the announcement and the entire ballroom erupted into a collective sigh.

The prodigal princess, finally taking her place.

Mak watched from his position in the back of the room, his hand wrapped around one of the stone pillars, decorated with an intricate twining vine of bronze. A thing of beauty. And only one of the many things in the palace he would happily tear apart in that moment.

Eva looked waxen, her expression serene, guarded. He feared she might have learned that from him. He couldn't spare a moment to look at the man standing at her side. He was unimportant. Mak wouldn't waste one moment when Eva was in his sight.

Then Bastian Van Saant, began to speak and Mak tightened his hold on the pillar. So easy to imagine he was squeezing the other man's neck. Far too easy. He talked about time-honored traditions, and uniting two powerful families. The unification of Komenia and Kyonos. He didn't speak of love. Of why Eva was essential. Why she was special.

Mak knew why. Wherever Eva went, she would bring brightness, a sort of sparkle that was unique to her. Unlike anyone else in the world. She would bring energy, humor and a bit of scandal. And he doubted Van Saant would appreciate any of that.

She was right. She was nothing more than an item to these men, to her fiancé, to her father. A stock to be bought and sold when the market price was right. Van Saant had gotten a hell of deal since the value on his recent purchase was down, thanks to the salacious stories in the news.

The very idea made bile rise in his throat. Eva was a pearl beyond price. If it were but a matter of selling every last possession to have her, he would. He would give up everything to have her.

But it was more than that.

It was the cost to her, that was the cost that was unacceptable.

Finally, Van Saant quit speaking and music began playing again. Bastian took Eva's hand and led her to the dance floor. Mak tightened his grip on the pillar, holding himself in place, willing himself not to cross the room and carry her out of it, just as he'd threatened to do at the casino so many weeks ago. Weeks that seemed like a lifetime ago.

Even if she ran from her fiancé's arms now, there was nothing. He could do nothing. Give her nothing. Nothing but the shell of a man, a shadow of who he'd once been.

For a brief time, she'd brought something more back into his life. She gave him light again, in that way only she could. But he would steal it all someday, if he let her keep giving.

He would leave her as dry as he was now.

The dancing couple turned and he caught Eva's eyes, saw a weight, a haunting sadness in the dark depths he'd never seen before. He saw how much this marriage would cost her and it made his stomach burn.

He released his hold on the pillar and felt sharp pain he hadn't been aware of. He looked at his palm, blood dripping from there down his wrist. There were thorns on the bronze vine. He hadn't even realized.

Physical pain was nothing in the face of the pain in his chest. It was almost welcome, because it helped dull the edge. He brushed his hand down his pant leg, not caring if he left a stain. This entire night would leave a stain inside him. Forever. Why not have a bit of external proof?

He walked out of the ballroom and into the corridor, his heart raging. His tie suddenly felt too tight, as if it was choking him. He tugged on the knot and cast it onto the floor, walking toward the front entrance.

The front of the palace was lit up by hundreds of lights

strung overhead. There were staff cars parked along the front, and even a horse-drawn carriage, as if it was a ball from a bloody fairy tale.

He stalked down the drive. He would have to come back. He was still working for the king. But he couldn't stay now. He couldn't bear to watch Eva with another man. With the man who would be bound to her for all of his life. The man who didn't know what a gift that was.

"Mak!"

He turned and saw Eva running to him, her skirt balled up in her fists, tugged up past her knees, showing delicate, glittery shoes that glinted in the lights.

"Mak, please stop!"

He did and so did she, a few feet in front of him, her breasts rising and falling in time with her breathing, her heavy eye makeup smeared down her cheeks.

"You left your tie," she said, her breathing heavy.

He noticed that she had the tie wadded up in the same hand that was gripping her skirt. "I have other black ties."

"I know."

He started to turn from her. "I'll be back, Eva, I'm just leaving for a while."

"Give me a reason, Mak," she said, her voice breaking. "Give me just one. I'll go and tell him it's off. I'll announce it to the whole damn country myself." She raised her hand to wipe a tear from her cheek, her fingers trembling.

He shook his head. "Don't. Don't do it for me, Eva."

"What other reason do I have?"

He closed the distance between them, taking a chance, a big chance, by touching her arm. "You're worth more than that. Do it because you deserve happiness. Because you deserve to live for more than this outdated idea of what honor is. You are more than a possession, you've said it to me many times, so show your father it's true. Those are good reasons, real reasons, to call it off. But don't do it for me. I'm not worth it."

"Yes you are," she said, her voice thick.

Pain burst through him. "No. I have nothing to give you. Nothing."

Eva looked at Mak, desperation gnawing at her. How could he see nothing in himself when she looked at him and saw her whole world.

"I don't care," she said, the words bursting from her. She didn't care about her pride, not in that moment. "Let me take care of you. Let me give to you. Take from me. Take it all, I don't care."

He advanced on her and wrapped his hand around her wrist, tugging her up against him. He dropped his head and kissed her lips, fiercely, intimately. Like a man who knew every inch of his lover. A man who was desperate. Desperate for her.

He pulled away from her abruptly, taking a step back. "No, Eva. Don't ask me to do that. Don't tempt me. My honor has its limits. I know the cost of those kinds of relationships. I had no choice in mine. The only sins committed belonged to me. You have no obligation to me. Don't sign yourself up for a life of me taking from you, because damn it, Eva, I'm tempted to take you up on it."

"Do. Please do." She said, desperation tugging at her.

"No. Because you want love. You deserve love and I can't." The words sounded broken, torn from him.

"I don't love Bastian, so what difference does it make?"

"Every difference. He wants you. I don't."

She looked at him, at his cold, dark eyes. And she knew he was lying. She also knew she couldn't drag the truth from him. This man, the love of her life. The man who had been a virgin at twenty-nine because he had chosen loyalty, strength, over any physical desire. And she knew he wouldn't break now.

"But I love you," she said. "And I don't love him."

Mak barely moved when she said the words, but she could tell they'd hit him. Hard. "All the more reason for me to walk away."

He turned. "Don't walk too far," she said. He looked back at her. "Aren't you doing security for my wedding?"

She watched a muscle in his jaw tick. "That's right. I'll see you then."

He turned away, cold as ice, composed as ever.

And every piece of her heart shattered, raining down like ash as it settled in her stomach. Nausea pervaded her body. She put a hand to her stomach, trying to fight the urge to vomit.

She looked down at the black silk tie, still in her hand. She felt as though she'd been left holding the glass slipper. Except she knew who it belonged to. She knew her perfect fit.

She walked over to the expansive grass lawn around the circular drive. She sat down, letting her dress fan out around her, and pressed the tie to her chest. Moisture seeped from the grass through her dress. She didn't care.

"Princess Evangelina?" One of the security guards approached her. "Are you all right?"

"I just need to think," she said. "Just a minute."

Do it for you.

Suddenly reality crashed in. She'd been unhappy for a long time, and she'd fought her fate like a rebellious teenager. By acting out, by causing a scene. And never once had she stood before her father and told him what she wanted from life. Never once taken a stand.

Because she'd been afraid. Afraid to take a definitive

stance. To say what she really wanted for fear of it being rejected. For fear of having herself rejected, really and truly.

"Well, it's sort of do or die now," she said.

She stood and brushed herself off. This gown didn't have a hope of being salvaged, not after all the action it had seen tonight. The thought brought an ache to her chest and a sad smile to her lips.

Too bad she hadn't done it sooner. Too bad she hadn't grown up a bit sooner.

She turned to look at the place Mak had last stood. Empty now.

"I'll do it for me," she said, not caring that the security guard probably thought she was losing it. Maybe she was, but it felt a whole lot more like she was finally getting it. "Thank you, Mak."

She headed back into the palace, a sense of triumph coming to help ease some of the ache in her body. Right now, she wouldn't think about what she'd lost. Later—she would grieve for it later.

Because right now she had to go and talk to her father.

CHAPTER FOURTEEN

THERE was no happiness in the bottom of a bottle of alcohol. Mak knew that for a fact. He also knew there was nothing more than a hole in his chest where his heart should be.

Eva had his heart.

He paced the length of his hotel room. He'd gotten a room in town, for the quietness. For a chance to think. He was still tied to this place. To this job.

To Eva. Honor, seeing his commitments through, that was just a thin veil. A facade to give him an excuse to stay where Eva was. To avoid leaving the country, making the ties feel severed permanently.

He walked to the mirror, braced his hands on the edges of the vanity. He looked at his reflection, and he hated the man he saw. "Coward," he said. "You are a coward."

The worst kind. He had let himself believe that all of his fear was for Eva, that he was afraid he would take too much from her. But he'd realized something in the twenty-four hours since he'd left her. That the love he felt for her had only ever given to both of them.

So his fear, the fear he had professed to feeling, was a lie, masking the real thing he was afraid of.

Of feeling pain again. Of opening himself up.

But he was open already. He was feeling already. Lost already. In Eva. In his love for her.

"I love her," he said to his hated reflection. He felt something crack in his chest. Felt so raw and exposed, but alone with that exposure, he felt new. He felt that he'd been given another chance. That his heart had started again.

She was engaged to another man. But she didn't love the other man. Maybe honor would have him stay away.

But love needed him to go to her. Now.

Freedom should feel more free than it did. It was the weight of missing Mak, that was what kept her from feeling total elation at her broken engagement.

It hadn't been easy, and her father hadn't been happy. But, for all his bluster, when she'd come in with confidence, when she'd laid out what she wanted, he'd told her he wouldn't force her into it.

He also didn't disown her. Didn't tell her to hand in her tiara.

She'd also explained her bad behavior, that she'd been trying to stop the engagement from happening without taking actual responsibility for it. That, combined with her flat denial of her involvement with either of the idiots from the casino, relieved him so much his anger fizzled.

It wasn't as though things were going to be perfect between them. He hadn't hugged her, or anything. But it was a step. A start. She'd asked for respect and she was on her way to earning it.

Still, she felt a solid ache in her chest that wouldn't go away. She missed Mak. Missed him more than she could express with words. It was awful. She wanted his arms around her at night, wanted to ride in the car with him when she went down to the city. Wanted to dance with him in the garden. Or just have dinner with him, she wasn't picky. She just wanted to be with him.

She walked out of her room and headed down the hall, toward the doors to the palace. She was going in to town with another security guard today, getting coffee, making a plan. She had a charity idea brewing, and since she was no longer being sent off into marriage she had some time to think about it.

She wanted to make sure that people with loved ones who needed long-term care, people like Mak, would have some sort of help from the get-go, so that the responsibility wouldn't fall all on them.

Thankfully, there would be no additional media circus today. At Bastian's request they were delaying the announcement of the broken engagement. That suited her fine. She couldn't handle being in the public eye. Not now. Not when she just wanted to hide away and lick her wounds.

Well, she wasn't going to let herself hide completely. She was going to make herself count. She was determined to.

A man in a black suit rounded one of the corners and her heart stopped. It might be a vision. A mirage. She usually saw them in her dreams, but a waking one didn't seem that odd. Which was telling.

"Mak?" she breathed.

His pace quickened. He was nearly running in the halls now and she couldn't keep her feet still. She went to greet him, throwing her arms around his neck as he wrapped his arms around her waist.

"I missed you so much," she said. She didn't care that last time they'd spoken he'd rejected her. It didn't matter now. Not in this moment. This was pure emotion, and she could feel it flowing from him too. Feel that his reaction was real, not something to keep from hurting her feelings.

He dropped to his knees in front of her and she looked over her shoulder, trying to see if anyone was walking by. "What are…"

"Marry me. Don't marry him," he ground out. "Marry

me, because I love you. I'm not perfect. I'm not a prince. I'm a widower who spent too many years living in the bitterness life gave me. I let it change me. I let it harden me. I was afraid to love, afraid of what it would cost me. Cost you. But then I realized that all your love has ever given me was happiness. More happiness than I've ever felt. I think it had just been so long since I felt the emotion I didn't recognize it."

"But…but…"

"I can't make you a queen, not in the eyes of the world. But I will treat you like one. I will give you everything I have to give."

She knelt down in front of him and put her hand on his face. "You…first of all, you make me happier than any man… than anyone ever. You make me feel so free. You make me feel like me. And I…I can never thank you enough for that."

"I make you happy?"

"So much. I broke the engagement. The night of the ball. I went and told my father I couldn't do it. Then I went to Bastian's hotel and I told him it was off. I don't think he was sorry. Because you were right. And you showed me that I… that I needed to grow up. And I did. So I am now free to accept the hand of any man I choose. And I choose you, Makhail Nabatov. Not in spite of your past, or the scars it's left. Those things have made you the man you are. The man I love."

He lowered his head. "I was a coward. It was easy to tell myself that I was afraid of taking too much from you. Because I've been there. But in truth, I was afraid to open myself. To find it in me to love. Imagine my surprise when I realized it was too late. It was so effortless to love you I almost didn't recognize it. You brought down my walls so easily, I hardly realized."

She laughed through her tears, cupped his chin and raised his face so he was looking at her. "You actually," she fumbled for her purse and unzipped it, taking out a length of black silk, "you saved me a trip into the city. You see, I found this, and I tried it on Bastian, but it didn't fit. And I was about to go searching to see if there was any man down in the shops it might fit…but…" She draped it over his shoulders. "You know, if looks like it fits you perfectly."

He laughed, a smile, a real smile, on his lips. He tugged her to him. "Ties are sort of one size fits all."

She shook her head. "That one's very special. It fits the one man who fits me."

"Eva, my love, how close I came to losing you." He leaned in and kissed her. "I am so sorry."

"I can handle you, as long as you can handle me," she said.

"More than. It's no chore."

"I feel the same way. I love you, you know," she said.

"I know." He reached into his pocket. "I have a ring for you."

"I'd love to see it…but…I think maybe after we spend some time in my bedroom."

He stood and took her hand, tugging her up with him. "You, my princess, are scandalous."

"I don't plan on changing, so I hope that's all right with you."

"It is. Don't ever change."

"You neither."

He took her hand and they walked toward her quarters. They would deal with her father, her brother, the rest of the world, later. Today was for them. And then, the rest of their lives.

"Hey, are you still going to do security for my wedding?" she asked.

He took her chin between his thumb and forefinger, a small smile on his lips. "I think I'll just be the groom at your wedding, and leave the rest to someone else."

"That sounds like a plan."

"I was so hoping that night in the garden wasn't our last kiss," he said, studying her face.

She stretched up on her toes and pressed her lips to his, lingering, reveling in the feel of him, the taste of him. Her Mak. Her future husband. "No, *agape mou,*" she said. "That wasn't the end of our kisses. That was only the beginning."

* * * * *

Mills & Boon® Hardback

July 2012

ROMANCE

The Secrets She Carried	Lynne Graham
To Love, Honour and Betray	Jennie Lucas
Heart of a Desert Warrior	Lucy Monroe
Unnoticed and Untouched	Lynn Raye Harris
A Royal World Apart	Maisey Yates
Distracted by her Virtue	Maggie Cox
The Count's Prize	Christina Hollis
The Tarnished Jewel of Jazaar	Susanna Carr
Keeping Her Up All Night	Anna Cleary
The Rules of Engagement	Ally Blake
Argentinian in the Outback	Margaret Way
The Sheriff's Doorstep Baby	Teresa Carpenter
The Sheikh's Jewel	Melissa James
The Rebel Rancher	Donna Alward
Always the Best Man	Fiona Harper
How the Playboy Got Serious	Shirley Jump
Sydney Harbour Hospital: Marco's Temptation	Fiona McArthur
Dr Tall, Dark...and Dangerous?	Lynne Marshall

MEDICAL

The Legendary Playboy Surgeon	Alison Roberts
Falling for Her Impossible Boss	Alison Roberts
Letting Go With Dr Rodriguez	Fiona Lowe
Waking Up With His Runaway Bride	Louisa George

Mills & Boon® Large Print

July 2012

ROMANCE

Roccanti's Marriage Revenge	Lynne Graham
The Devil and Miss Jones	Kate Walker
Sheikh Without a Heart	Sandra Marton
Savas's Wildcat	Anne McAllister
A Bride for the Island Prince	Rebecca Winters
The Nanny and the Boss's Twins	Barbara McMahon
Once a Cowboy...	Patricia Thayer
When Chocolate Is Not Enough...	Nina Harrington

HISTORICAL

The Mysterious Lord Marlowe	Anne Herries
Marrying the Royal Marine	Carla Kelly
A Most Unladylike Adventure	Elizabeth Beacon
Seduced by Her Highland Warrior	Michelle Willingham

MEDICAL

The Boss She Can't Resist	Lucy Clark
Heart Surgeon, Hero...Husband?	Susan Carlisle
Dr Langley: Protector or Playboy?	Joanna Neil
Daredevil and Dr Kate	Leah Martyn
Spring Proposal in Swallowbrook	Abigail Gordon
Doctor's Guide to Dating in the Jungle	Tina Beckett

0612 GEN STD LP

Mills & Boon® Hardback

August 2012

ROMANCE

Contract with Consequences	Miranda Lee
The Sheikh's Last Gamble	Trish Morey
The Man She Shouldn't Crave	Lucy Ellis
The Girl He'd Overlooked	Cathy Williams
A Tainted Beauty	Sharon Kendrick
One Night With The Enemy	Abby Green
The Dangerous Jacob Wilde	Sandra Marton
His Last Chance at Redemption	Michelle Conder
The Hidden Heart of Rico Rossi	Kate Hardy
Marrying the Enemy	Nicola Marsh
Mr Right, Next Door!	Barbara Wallace
The Cowboy Comes Home	Patricia Thayer
The Rancher's Housekeeper	Rebecca Winters
Her Outback Rescuer	Marion Lennox
Monsoon Wedding Fever	Shoma Narayanan
If the Ring Fits...	Jackie Braun
Sydney Harbour Hospital: Ava's Re-Awakening	Carol Marinelli
How To Mend A Broken Heart	Amy Andrews

MEDICAL

Falling for Dr Fearless	Lucy Clark
The Nurse He Shouldn't Notice	Susan Carlisle
Every Boy's Dream Dad	Sue MacKay
Return of the Rebel Surgeon	Connie Cox

Mills & Boon® Large Print

August 2012

ROMANCE

A Deal at the Altar	Lynne Graham
Return of the Moralis Wife	Jacqueline Baird
Gianni's Pride	Kim Lawrence
Undone by His Touch	Annie West
The Cattle King's Bride	Margaret Way
New York's Finest Rebel	Trish Wylie
The Man Who Saw Her Beauty	Michelle Douglas
The Last Real Cowboy	Donna Alward
The Legend of de Marco	Abby Green
Stepping out of the Shadows	Robyn Donald
Deserving of His Diamonds?	Melanie Milburne

HISTORICAL

The Scandalous Lord Lanchester	Anne Herries
Highland Rogue, London Miss	Margaret Moore
His Compromised Countess	Deborah Hale
The Dragon and the Pearl	Jeannie Lin
Destitute On His Doorstep	Helen Dickson

MEDICAL

Sydney Harbour Hospital: Lily's Scandal	Marion Lennox
Sydney Harbour Hospital: Zoe's Baby	Alison Roberts
Gina's Little Secret	Jennifer Taylor
Taming the Lone Doc's Heart	Lucy Clark
The Runaway Nurse	Dianne Drake
The Baby Who Saved Dr Cynical	Connie Cox

Discover Pure Reading Pleasure with

Visit the Mills & Boon website for all the latest in romance

 Buy all the latest releases, backlist and eBooks

Find out more about our authors and their books

Join our community and chat to authors and other readers

Free online reads from your favourite authors

Win with our fantastic online competitions

Sign up for our free monthly eNewsletter

Tell us what you think by signing up to our reader panel

Rate and review books with our star system

www.millsandboon.co.uk

 Follow us at twitter.com/millsandboonuk

Become a fan at facebook.com/romancehq